The Broken House

Martyn Carey

—

Index

—

New Life

Spring should be a time of hope and renewal, but the first green shoots of this year were growing through the eye sockets of the skull I found in my garden.

My house isn't very big, just an old cottage on the edge of a village that would really like to be a small town, but it doesn't have the legs. There would have been roses around the door – had been – but one of the things I brought with me, apart from my idiot dog Boswell, were the least green thumbs known to man. My daughter says I'm the only person she knows who can kill lichen.

The last owner of the cottage had been dead keen on the whole 'borrowed landscape' deal, so she'd removed the trees and hedges at the far end of the long narrow garden. The person who planted them had

—

been awfully fond of rowan.

The loose, open forest beyond was rich with ancient, four-square oaks, towering ash trees and psychopathic blackthorns that seemed intent on attacking me every time I went in there. It was hard not to take it personally.

But the rowans were now gone, and so was the hawthorn hedge, dug out and burnt in the brief time she'd been in the house. She'd enjoyed her retirement for only three months before her heart gave out one moonlit night.

The skull as probably a fox, certainly something dog-like with big crushing teeth. I'd found the rest of the skeleton too, stretched out over the place where the hedge had been, as if it had been stripped of all its flesh in the act of leaping out of the forest.

Skeletons don't bother me, so I'd gathered it all

—

up into a paper sack and buried it out in the woods beyond the hedge line. The chilly spring wind shuffled around me as I dug, but I was still sweating by the time I'd finished; it seemed to be a tremendous effort. I probably should have left all of it for the insects, but it was just dry bones and would have wrecked the mower when I, inevitably having forgotten about it, finally got around to cutting the grass.

The mouse skeletons I'd found – probably mouse, I'm not an expert on small quadrupedal mammalian anatomy – I'd just chucked into the bushes on the edge of the trees. I'd thought the whole 'green thumb' thing was only to do with plants, but I was now starting to wonder if it extended to small animals too.

*

—

I found it hard to sleep that night, probably because of the ripe cheese and old ale I'd had for supper. Resisting the urge to belch the alphabet – the pinnacle of achievement when I was at primary school – I made myself some tea and sat in what the estate agent had called 'the lounge'. My grandmother would have called it 'the parlour' and kept it for best. My dad had called it the 'back room' and filled it with fishing gear and trout flies and my disappointing school reports.

For me it was books, piles and lines and stacks of books, because not even I can kill books. It also contains the one plant that I still own, a cactus named Hector, recommended by an understanding friend on the grounds that it was so dormant that I wouldn't be able to tell if it was dead or not, which might break the jinx. But as I can't tell if it's dead, I don't know if it's worked.

We weren't far enough into spring for the nights to be even vaguely warm, but the bite of winter had

—

faded in the last week or so. The moonlight showed the garden, in all its lack of glory, and the forest beyond. It would be nice to say it loomed, but it was too far away. It would be nice to say it brooded, but it was too thin, the trees too well spaced.

From my bedroom window, I could see some ancient regularity to it. I saw movement too but I didn't move. The trees were home to lots of small animals, but this was the first time I'd been wakeful in the night so I'd not seen them before. I finished my tea and took my heavy eyelids to my modest bed and fell deeply asleep until well after sunrise.

The whole regularity thing puzzled me, because I couldn't see it the next morning, at least not until I went back upstairs and looked from my bedroom window again. It was definitely there, an almost circular pattern, and I decided that I would go and have a look.

I heard the tiny deer before I saw it, a squeaking

—

and thrashing beyond the stand of brambles. I walked very carefully around it, to see a Muntjac tangled in the wire fence, or the remnants of a wire fence. It took me several minutes of walking slowly and speaking in a calm voice before I could get close enough to help. The animal was sensible enough to let me untangle it, but it still ran off before I could check it for injury.

So I looked at the fence, registering for the first time just how old it was. The post that had rotted through was otherwise solid and heavy, the kind you'd expect to outlast the wire hanging from it. But a crackling as I walked made me look closer. Buried in the leaf litter was the remains of a woven fence, twigs interlaced to create a barrier. Or rather a marker, because from the size, I would have been able to step over it without endangering my chances of becoming a father. I thought that the wire had been a quick replacement after rot had taken the older one.

—

I traced it for a while, and it curved around in a circle until a more modern track erased it completely. I decided to stop following it. The rain dripping down the back of my neck could also have been a factor.

So, I looked further for the circularity of the trees and spotted it quite quickly. Ash mostly, stark and grey against the pellucid spring sky, they were in three concentric circles with scant undergrowth in between. They had to have been planted like that, or at least thinned out to create the effect.

The next step was to visit the dead centre of the circles. The thin undergrowth made it quite easy, right up to the point where I fell into a ditch. It was about waist deep and full of whole winter's worth of slimy things and suspicious beetles, and I went in face first. Seriously yuck and ewww and all that stuff. Mumbling imprecations about whoever had left it lying around in the middle of the forest, I clambered out. Then

—

I realised it was circular and on a line that matched that of the trees. Wary in case these came in threes as well, I set off again, but the ground remained unevenly firm until I located the centre of all this circling.

Rotting stumps indicated that an impressive level of decimation had been visited upon the space some time earlier. It was an otherwise disappointingly empty space, scrubby grass and errant twigs and a pervasive smell of something in an advanced state of decay. I'd been expecting something, like maybe a standing stone.

I mean, a lying down stone would have done, but there was just grass and weeds and that horrible stink. It often smells a bit rural around the house, but this was foul. Just then it started to snow. In spring, without a cloud in the sky. It wasn't snow, it was ash, but I couldn't see any smoke anywhere, so I had no idea where it was coming from. A flake landed in my mouth. It tasted of sweat and blood and something like hot

—

metal. I left, because I'd had quite enough of being weirded out for one day.

*

The smell was in the house by the next morning, and Boswell was hiding by the front door, trying to breathe through his ears. I tracked the stench down to the boots I had been wearing the previous day. I wasn't sure I'd ever be able to wear them again, which was a shame because they were really comfortable.

Today hadn't the clear brightness of the previous day. The sluggishness of the broken night put me in an odd frame of mind. Now the trees did loom, as if they'd shuffled closer to the end of the garden during the night. They present a dark barrier as the sun fitfully forced its way through the fog that deadened all the sound. Boswell didn't want to go into the garden, let alone for a walk, but I forced him outside for just long enough that he didn't make a mess on the carpet. When we came in he hid behind the big chair in the front room, the one where I usually sit to watch TV. I hadn't seen him like this since the last National Pet Frightening Day – sorry, bonfire night.

Mrs Verdean, who lives next door, gave me such a grudging greeting when I was in the front garden that I immediately apologised for the terrible smell. She seemed to have no idea what I was talking about.

"Your dog," she said, "has he been loose in the forest recently?"

"No," I said. "He won't go in there. Why?"

"There was a lot of disturbance last night."

"That was definitely not him. Boswell's too lazy to chase anything that moves faster than his food bowl."

She didn't look convinced, but Boswell is not young and when she stroked his greying head she

—

smiled a little and it seemed to reassure her.

"Did you investigate?" I asked. She shook her head, so I told her about the Muntjac. "I'll go and have a look later. Do you know who owns the land? Maybe we could ask them to clear the wire away?"

She didn't know, but Boswell wanted to go back inside, so I turned back to the house just as the fine drizzle began.

After a quick cup of tea to defrost my fingers I went down the garden and into the trees. It didn't take me long to find what was left of the Muntjac, half eaten on the forest floor. Foxes again, no doubt, but sad all the same. I could see the marks in the fur on its legs that told me it was the same one that I'd rescued. I couldn't see what had killed it. I was still nervous, and I could hear Boswell whining anxiously, so I left it alone.

*

—

Boswell wasn't in for breakfast this morning. I don't know how he got out, but I can see him in the garden. My heart hopes he's fallen asleep in the fitful sunshine, but my head doesn't agree. I don't want to go and find out.

*

I buried Boswell before the foxes got to him, weeping as I dug a hole by the hedge. The soil seemed powdery and sterile, all the roots sere and fragile, snapping at the least touch of the spade. I made him a stone box to lie in, using some paving slabs I found, because I didn't want him dug up. The silent flood of soil filling the space, covering his body, took my heart with it, and I sat in the lounge looking down the garden until the light finally faded and Boswell was at peace.

—

Mrs Verdean was sympathetic when I told her, but mentioned more disturbances in the night. I hadn't heard them, but I didn't doubt her word. I looked, but Boswell's grave was undisturbed, and I couldn't see anything new in the garden. I didn't go any further.

The forest could take care of itself – I didn't want to borrow its landscape any longer. I went back to the house and hired someone to replant the hawthorn hedge and fill the bottom of the garden with rowan trees.

When I'd finished, I looked at Hector the Cactus. The tiny spots of mould told me that whatever had got Boswell was now in the house. I don't know if the new trees will be planted soon enough to save me.

—

Unstitched in Time

I became temporally unstable on the fifth day of the Falling Stars in the fourth quarter of the sixth year of the King - or a wet Tuesday in May, depending on your point of view.

I'd been sitting in my cubicle at work, when I found myself in a totally different place. The land had a kind of bucolic desolation, a country where autumn has the air of being permanent. The trees reached upward, like a cluster of bare wires, into a blue sky that had an odd tinge of bronze to it.

A lot of people milled around over by a stone building in the distance, in that 'smashed anthill' way that distance can give to a restless crowd. I wasn't sure where 'over there' was; I wasn't even sure where 'here' was for that matter. All I knew for certain was that 'here'

—

didn't have any chairs, so I fell over on the soggy grass in an undignified, confused and, startled heap.

While the place didn't have chairs, it did have sheep, and several wandered over to look at me, making the 'blart' noise that people who live in towns – and the writers of children's books – think sounds like 'baaa'. I sat up with a jerk when the nearest one opened its mouth, because I was sure that I could see fangs. I tried to scramble to my feet and then, just as suddenly, I was back in my cubicle, facing a computer screen with a fatuous corporate message floating across it.

"That was weird," I said, catching the eye of Jenny, who sits opposite me.

"What was?"

"I dropped off for a second…" her eyes flashed a warning and I saw our supervisor bearing down on me with the inevitability of a super tanker whose captain has fallen asleep. Eric – known as Grunthose the

—

Magnificent, due an unfortunate trouser habit – was looming. He liked looming.

"Did you say you dropped off?" His voice was pinched and nasal and he was, as usual, looking for an excuse to be annoyed. Most of us lived on coffee, but Eric lived on irritation and spite.

"No Eric, I said I dropped this." I held up my pen as evidence.

"I see." He looked at me and sniffed. "Your appearance is not in keeping with the standards expected of this department," he went on. "I shall be watching you in future – be told." He pointed his finger at me in a manner he probably thought was magisterial but came out as petulant. He swept off with a swirl of his silk-lined black cape – or would have done if he'd been wearing one. I suspect that he'd love to be able to.

Jenny bent her head over her keyboard, so I decided not to continue the conversation. An odour

—

made itself known to me as I opened another file. It didn't smell like Eric, and I knew it wasn't me. I set the logging controls for a break and went to the toilet.

I was wet around the trousers, with grass stains on my elbows and something on the bottom of my shoe that was giving off a penetrating miasma that made my eyes water. I began to wonder how far I'd dropped when I dropped off.

*

It happened again that night, while I was flopped out on the couch at home watching 'Strictly Britain's Got Talent Factor on Ice' or something equally inane. I didn't think I had been anywhere near sleep– even I can't drop off while shouting abuse at the television – and then suddenly I was inside a castle. A real proper turrety sort of castle with fires burning in scones – no,

—

sorry, sconces – and no sign of a cash machine or a Wi-Fi connection anywhere.

I fell over again, of course, and cracked my elbow on the authentic stone-flagged floor. Then I heard footsteps coming down the corridor, the sort of martial tramp that film makers spend a fortune in special effects sound suites to create.

Here it was provided free of charge by eight men who were either guards or had a serious leather and chain mail fixation. By the time they arrived I was hiding. Voices suggested that more people were coming, so I stepped out of the shadow and into the doorway of an adjacent room.

Which, unfortunately, wasn't empty. There was a four-poster bed with hangings, and it was occupied. In the back of mind, I suppose I had vaguely hoped for a comely maiden in a diaphanous nightdress who would swoon at my entrance. Not a chance.

—

It was, I had realised, bloody freezing in the castle, so even if it had been a comely maiden she would have been in bed socks and a ton of blankets. But it wasn't, it was a man. I have no idea about the bed socks, but he wasn't doing any kind of swooning. He reared up in the bed like I'd stuck a needle in his bum, and stared for a second.

"Not again," he said under his breath. He wasn't speaking English, but I could understand him and annoyed sounds the same any language.

"Guards," he shouted in a voice that filled the room. The sound of running feet occurred and I looked for another exit. There was only a narrow window which I knew – don't ask me how – was just wide enough for me to get stuck in.

"Um…" I said. Sparkling wit and repartee have never been my strong point, but I can normally manage a coherent sentence. Not in this dream.

—

"When are you people going to leave me alone?" The man sounded more peeved than anything, and certainly not scared. But then, why would he be? The door slammed back and several people with unkind intentions grabbed me. A long, completely plain, dagger swung toward my face. I grabbed at it, ignoring the cut on my arm this earned me, and pushed it away.

The guard jerked it back toward me, and the fact my arms are about as strong as boiled string meant that he overpowered me with ease. I ducked and, to my considerable relief, woke up.

But not on the couch. Later I worked it out – the distance and direction I travelled in the dream matched the distance and direction in this world. This could be very useful if I could harness it – no bank vault would be safe from me. But I had a more immediate problem to deal with. When I woke up I was on the landing outside

—

the flat, in my boxers and a t-shirt with a cut arm, a long dagger and no door key.

I hid the dagger under the carpet then woke up Mrs Tebbutt next door. I told her I thought I'd heard an odd noise outside and had come out to investigate, while getting ready to go out, and had managed to lock myself out. She sighed, shook her head and gave me the spare key.

*

The dagger was a problem. Any of the other parts of the dream I could just about explain away – I dreamt of being wet because I was wet. I dreamt of a bedroom because the couch is an uncomfortable place to fall asleep. But a damn great steel dagger, with my blood still on it, was something I couldn't explain.

Nor the deep bruises around my wrist from the

—

guard's grip and the cut on my arm. Suddenly an interesting dream had become a nightmare that I couldn't think of a way to escape from.

I had to conclude that it was real, all of it – not a dream and not a sign that some of the recreational narcotics I tried when I was younger were repeating on me like old cheese. And that I was probably going to go there again at some random interval. So, what should I do? Well, go ready for whatever I might come across, I suppose. What would I need?

Appropriate clothing and footwear would be a must – warm and hardwearing. The dagger, of course, and some items that could be traded for food. Some food. I'd try for some solar powered technology, just see if it worked - I could be the most important man in the world if I could get a calculator to function. A book on basic technology maybe; soap and toothpaste; a medical kit of some kind; a compass; a watch; lots of painkillers;

—

coffee; and all sorts of other things, all of which seemed to be vital. It made for a very large rucksack, and of course I had to carry it all the time, be touching it, everywhere because I never knew when I would er...go there.

I don't think the police believed me.

Access All Areas

Her ring casually drew a long furrow of blood down my forearm, and I jerked back sharply. It looked as if it had been dipped in red ink.

"Oh sorry," said the woman sitting next to me. "Did I scratch you? Sorry." She lifted my arm and looked at it. I felt a tiny thrill at the contact, and a curious muttering stuttered around the coffee shop. Newly arrived in the department, Dr Lily James was beautiful and aloof in equal measure.

"It'll be fine," I said. "I'll just get it cleaned and put a plaster on it." It would be an exaggeration to say it was painful, but it was certainly uncomfortable, and felt like more than just a single line of damage.

"No," said Lily, running her forefinger along the underside of my forearm, "it'll be fine." She smiled again

—

and turned her back to her coffee. The diamond had a tiny red stain on the point, which she wiped away with a quick touch of her tongue. Now the scratch felt...odd, but whatever else, I didn't want to get blood on my clothes, so I headed for the medical room.

I ran the water into the sink until it was warm and then tentatively rinsed my arm. The line of scarlet blood held on stubbornly for a few seconds before dissolving, and the sink was briefly touched with odd shade of green. I wondered what kind of cleaning materials they were using now – I'd never seen that before.

Then I carefully patted my arm dry, only to find that there wasn't a scratch after at all, just a long, dark line that faded as I looked. Suspecting that I had just had an elaborate trick played on me – even in the hallowed and intellectual realms of the university I was considered a bit of a nerd. So I decided that I needed to do work more than I needed to drink more of the ghastly ersatz

—

coffee they foist on us in the canteen.

I was sure that Lily was having a good laugh at my expense – but at least I hadn't panicked or flapped about it. I headed off, leaving the rest of the researchers in physical sciences to their silly games.

*

Lily found me again an hour or so later, peering at a large screen covered in small text and big equations. "Hello," she said.

I glanced up. "Hi." She'd only been at the university for about a week, and her appearance had sparked considerable interest and comment in most male members of staff below the age of dead. She'd paid them no attention, burying herself deeply in her work, the kind of physics that sounds like the more excitable parts of ancient religious texts.

—

"I wanted to ask you something about your work…" she began, leaning forward. I was cautious after that earlier business, but caution isn't a reason to be unfriendly. "What bit in particular?" She pointed to an equation on the screen I had in front of me. Even printed eight point it was the size of a tennis ball, and I wasn't sure that it was right. The more complicated the equation, the longer it takes to get it spot on. But it was odd, because even now some of the numbers in it were changing as I watched, which shouldn't be able to happen, as if the things it was describing weren't stable.

"The transfer equation?" I shook my head. "Sorry, but I think I've made a mistake somewhere further back, because if it's correct then energy is being destroyed." Which, in case you don't know, isn't possible. Changed in form or state yes, but not destroyed.

"I don't think it's being destroyed," said Lily. "I think it's going somewhere else, somewhere outside the

—

system described in the equation."

"But this is based on universal constants," I said. "If it's right it will apply everywhere in the universe." I began to think she was taking the piss again.

"My point exactly," she said, touching me briefly on the shoulder and hip swaying her way out of the room. A lab coat shouldn't look that good on anybody.

I felt something moving on my hand, and looked down to see the long scratch had opened again and blood was dripping from my fingertips onto the floor in front of me.

*

I normally sleep well. I run home from the lab most nights, which is the best part of 5 miles, as a cure for sitting on my backside all day. But that night I slept really badly, stretched on the rack of dreams I couldn't

—

recall coherently.

That damned transfer equation featured prominently, and the components glowed briefly and brightly, like rainbow lightning. At the heart of it was a description of the energy state – $\Delta J = \Delta t^4 - \Delta t^2 \ (\infty \geq x \ \sqrt{t1})$ and so on – and the little bit of it that described it's resting state – when it became potential energy – glowed so brightly that it hurt my eyes, even as I dreamt.

I plunged towards it and the equation shattered into glowing fragments. I dived into it, twisting like an otter playing, watching the numbers dance around and rearranging themselves into ways that made no sense mathematically. I'm not talking calculus, which rarely appears to make sense; this was 2+2=7 sort of wrong.

It took a moment to realise that the numbers weren't floating, but were being written on a sheet of glass in front of me. More, were writing themselves on the glass. There seemed to a deeper meaning hidden

—

somewhere in this dream, like Watson's DNA spiral staircase, so I pushed forward – and the glass shattered. Numbers fell around me like crystal rain and I found myself falling forwards.

I dropped into horror. The landscape was black and broken, ravaged by fire, with rats the size of dogs scurrying around beneath the inky sky. Rivers of steam rolled through the turgid air, and my skin felt sticky and gritty at the same time. I stood on the rough ground and felt the waves of heat coming off the rivers of grey sludge that crept past me. On the far horizon there were buildings, but closer I could see movement, which became a creature with great wings beating spirals into the smoky air as the vaguely human shaped creatures floated down towards me.

I wasn't brought up a Catholic, but my culture is shot through with their harrowing and self-destructive vision of life after death, and I wondered why on earth I

—

was dreaming about it; I never had before. Fortunately there was a marked absence of damned souls being unimaginatively tortured by thuggish demons, so eternal screaming wasn't providing the soundtrack.

The flying figures came closer, stooping like hawks on great bat-like wings, and then crashing to the stony ground with a loud grunt. The finer points of a controlled landing were clearly not in their skill set.

"What is this?" The taller of the two hissed in a puzzled voice full of sibilants. They spoke English, or at least I heard English. "Why has it been sent?"

I was amused, but puzzled by the word 'sent'. I'd fallen through an inaccurate equation to get here – that hardly counted as being sent.

"Find it's sending mark Noorun." The other one's voice was more guttural, and the tone suggested a being substantially smarter than the first.

Noorun, wingy fangy beast number 1, grabbed

—

my hand and peered at my palm. "There's no mark Daldd," it grunted. "Can I eat it?" I think this was supposed to be a joke, but I wasn't sure.

"No," said Daldd, with exaggerated patience. "Look at its arms." The tone was familiar, the slight exasperation of dealing with someone who's not very bright. I felt my arm twisted, not at all gently, and it grunted. "Is here."

It was pointing to a long line incised down my arm. In the vague light, it had tick marks on the sides, like barbed wire or Ogham or another one of those 'scratched on stone' languages, scripts that avoided curved lines.

Daldd, wingy fangy beast number 2, peered, and its outstandingly ugly face – the unhappy bastard child of an irritated warthog and a dyspeptic walrus, with added fangs – crumpled into what had to be a frown. Either that, or it had decided to fold its face in half for

—

some reason.

"Why would Maja send this here, not just come?" Its voice had a quiet, musing tone, then it looked at me. "You go now. Tell Maja that we've got the message. We'll all be ready when the time comes." I looked at it, bemused by what was happening. "Did you hear me?" It reached out with a finger the thickness of my leg and prodded me in the chest with hard, grating nails. "Can it speak?" I felt a sharp pain and the dampness of blood on my shirt.

And then I woke up, seeing dawn's far too early light creeping under the edge of the curtains. I sat up, feeling strangely weak. I smelled smoke in my hair and coughed. I looked around the room. Nothing was on fire, but I remembered that the people next door had been burning early pruning's the day before. So my subconscious had grabbed the implications of the smell and populated my dreams accordingly. The cough put

—

the word 'tea' into my head.

So I put the kettle on. While I was looking out at the starless night I noticed a dark stain on my pyjama top. This proved to be blood, seeping from a triangular tear just over my heart. Which explained why I'd dreamt of the injury, but not how I'd got it.

*

Lily was sitting beside my desk when I got into the office, reclining in a posture that was too uncomfortable to be languorous and too revealing to be accidental. She looked like a lady of uncertain virtue in a Raymond Chandler novel.

"Morning," I said, perching my extra-large, double strength, heavily sugared coffee on the corner of my desk. I'd dropped off on the couch at around 5.30, but my chest was sore and inflamed, so I was tense and

—

terse and stuff like that.

"Well hello," she said, "and did we have a good time last night?"

"Last night?"

She sat up. "You look awful, you've enough caffeine in there to kick-start a dead horse and you have the breath of a thousand camels. Was it fun? More importantly, was it worth it?" I explained about bad dreams and so forth, while making serious inroads into my coffee, and she smiled softly. Her lips were unreasonably curved. "You sure it wasn't a premonition or something? Do you have premonitions?"

"No," I said as the sugar and caffeine worked their magic on me. "It was just a weird dream. Noorun and Daldd treated me like a strange creature from an unfamiliar eco-system, like someone from Wolverhampton finding a kangaroo in their back garden. They sent me back with a message."

—

"A message?"

"Tell Maja I've got the message," I replied. "We'll all be ready when the time comes. It's amazing what your subconscious comes up with, isn't it?"

Lily nodded absently, then swung several yards of shapely leg off the edge of my desk and stood up. "I need to talk to you about your equations again. Pin-hole access isn't going to be enough."

"Pin-hole access?" I had no idea what she meant.

"Look," she said, grabbing my keyboard and starting to type rapidly. We use a specialist system that makes creating large and complex equations relatively easy, and can even give you a running result if you ask it to. It was groaning by the time she'd finished, and although the equation was elegant and well-structured it was also wrong. I couldn't see why for a moment, then I realised she'd made a mistake early on – I'm not being unreasonably critical, because it's hard to get something

—

this eye-wateringly complicated dead right first time. But this was her specialist field and was something she should be able to do with her eyes closed; it looked like she had.

"The energy transfer in your equation was in the *Tau Delta* range," she said, "but if you invert the ΩT^4 function with respect to the ΔT^4 function…"

She was right, of course. Lily is a full Professor from a very respected Australian university, and my boss was so chuffed when she accepted the offer to come here…so it was hard for me to point out that although what she had done was completely correct, it was based on a false starting assumption. But I'm only an Associate Professor, a lesser breed, so I waited to be enlightened.

She saw my look and smiled. "Just go with me on this," she said, her violet eyes twinkling. And so my day passed with complex mathematics and coffee in equal measure, and I made very careful note of what Lily did.

—

Having 'Prof. L.J. James Pers Comm' as a citation would give my research paper a huge credibility boost.

*

I dreamt again, the same place again, but not exactly the same. When I arrived, I was near the buildings, looming black ones like the tower blocks of the damned. More of the fangy wingy creatures were moving around them, streaming through what I'd like to call a 'dread portal', but looked more like the door to my office. It did squeak, but it wasn't a tortured, eldritch sound, just the noise of something that needs oiling.

There was no sign of numbnuts and his mate, but several wingy fangy beasts looked at me curiously. One approached me, but I held up my arm to display the line on my forearm and it stopped, suddenly casual and unconcerned, like a suspicious security guard finally

—

spotting your id badge and trying to look like he wasn't checking up on you in the first place.

I wasn't frightened this time, although the whole 'dungeon dimensions' bit was no less obvious. Inky sky, bat winged creatures, roiling smoke, distant volcanoes, everything my imagination could provide. Nothing came near me, and after a peaceful if worrying few moments in this unpleasant nether world, I woke up.

'Nice place to visit but I wouldn't want to live there', I thought as I settled back to sleep. Getting up at 5 o'clock once is OK, but I'd already had one short night and it was only half past two. I was asleep again in moments, and I didn't dream– well, not about that place. There was one involving Lily, black lace, ice cream and silk sheets, but I'll keep that one to myself.

*

—

Next day I thought Lily must have been listening to my dreams because I couldn't shake her off. She sat by me, porting her work onto my system and combining her calculations with mine in a way that made... I was going to say 'no sense', but they kind of did, in an odd way. Again, change the starting conditions, and they would be fine.

But the starting conditions were to do with energy transitions through n dimensional space, something not normally considered possible. Her assumption was that dimensions were not separate entities but intermingled quantum states, once more with energy transfers permitted, which they aren't.

In the end, we came up with an equation that made sense mathematically, provided that you granted the variables. As far as I could see this wasn't anything more than a fascinating exercise in maths and an opportunity to sit close to the most gorgeous woman in

—

the university. It did my *kudos* a lot of good, even if not my blood pressure. She stared at the screen in silence for ages. "I'd never thought I'd find someone who could do this," she said to herself. "Maybe it will work this time."

"So now what?" I asked as the lights started to go out in other parts of the building.

"Are you free this evening?"

"Yes." I tried not to sound too eager, but positive and enthusiastic can get you quite a long way.

"Good. Meet me behind the…" she trailed off, eyes distant.

"Bike sheds?" I offered, which earned me a prod from a finger like a wood screw.

"Second car park. We need a bit of open space. Half an hour. Bring your laptop." She swung up onto her feet and I watched her walking away, her stride unconsciously enticing. I hadn't thought she'd want to be somewhere so public, but, hey, I was making a wall

—

of assumptions here anyway.

*

I sat on a tree stump and waited. Lily arrived five minutes later, wearing one of those paper suits the police use when they're doing forensics. This one was blue. Her hair was loose and she was wearing the plain diamond ring that had cut my arm.

"Hello," I said, rising. She smiled, but it was a dead thing, never touching her eyes, yet she seemed eager. She'd brought some long sticks with her, newly cut branches with the sap still bleeding from the broken ends. I wondered what she was expecting to happen.

"Just stay there," she said. She crouched down to drive the sticks into the ground. As the suit tightened across her thighs I could see that she wasn't wearing anything underneath it. This was becoming more weird

—

and less erotic with every passing moment.

Having created a frame, she turned to me. "We'll need that equation now," she said. Her voice was less mellifluous than before and my hands were moving to obey before my brain had a chance to say 'hey, hang on a minute'."

The diamond on her finger glowed and the space between the sticks became matt black, sucking the remnants of the sunlight into it, swirling like inky water going down a plug hole. The equation came up on the screen and Lily somehow reached out and pulled it off the monitor and threw it at the frame. There was a sudden chill and it changed, opening like a camera lens. Beyond it I could see the dark city, and now there was a crowd of wingy fangy things. They looked poised, like an invading army ready to strike, and I tried to cry out, but a gesture from Lily silenced me.

I heard the paper of Lily's suit tearing and got a

—

brief glimpse of rounded and exciting flesh before her skin hardened and darkened and her face transformed into the sickeningly familiar 'crumpled warthog', and wings unfurled from non-longer shapely shoulders.

"What the… are you going to invade or something? Did I just help you make a portal so your people could take over the world?"

No-longer-Lily turned to me. "No," it said softly. Its voice was so full wistful longing that I felt tears. "I just wanted to go home."

Lily stepped through, into the waiting, welcoming arms and the portal collapsed into ashes.

—

The Road from Darriel

We had been on the old traders' route from Pallin
to Darriel for three days. The wagon creaked as it
rumbled over the path, once rutted in the summers' heat
but now uncomfortably close to a mire atop the few
stones that remained of the old Imperial Road. The road
builders had been an old man's tale in my grandfather's
time, and few people had the time, energy or skill to
maintain the roads, even if they wanted to.

Sur Garrett, the Administrator of Pallin, certainly
wouldn't. He didn't care if you had to wade knee deep
as long as the string of wagons bringing food and trinkets
to the peacocks of the Administrators Court continued to
arrive on time.

"We should stop," said Gwen, "it'll be dark in
half a span and I'd like to set camp while there's still

—

some light left." She glanced around. "Nice to find somewhere dry for tonight."

I nodded and pulled the cart off the road into a stand of sheltering trees above the flooded landscape bedside the road. I raised my flat hand to the sun – she was right, the copper-red orb sat in the centre of my palm when the edge of my smallest finger touched the horizon. Half a span. In Pallin they would call that an hour, but on the road we've little use for clocks, even if we could find one that could survive the jolting.

For folks like us, 'which half of the day' was usually good enough, and we had the usual time songs for short durations. I always used 'The Lay of the Ash Tree' for boiling eggs – they come out just the way I like them. I have to sing the chorus twice more for Gwen's.

She cleared her throat in a pointed manner. "Tobias, are you going to be communing with the sun much longer? It's just that we need fire wood, or we'll

—

be having a cold supper. Again," she added. Last night we'd had to sleep in the cart, surrounded by water, because the only bit of dry ground we'd been able to find had only just been big enough for the horses to stand on.

I smiled and headed off into the trees. Damp wood there was aplenty, and deep-litter tinder too, but larger dry pieces were hard to find. I scooped up a selection to range around the fire to dry, at least a little, before we burned them. If we didn't do that we would all be kippered by the smoke within minutes. The horses would probably object more strongly than us.

Fern and Bracken had been pulling our wagon for more than five years, and probably knew the way to Pallin market better than I did.

I set the wood down by the shallow fire pit that Gwen had dug, sorted through the tinder I'd found under the leaf litter and had the fire crackling within

—

a few seconds. Steam started to rise from even the smallest twigs, and Gwen sighed.

"Get the sack Tobias, or this will be gone out before we can dry enough wood to feed it." As this fire was where I would make our supper, warm the mash for the horses and provide us with all the heat we would get for the whole soggy night, I quickly moved to get it. Inside we kept our rapidly dwindling supply of what the Mayor of Darriel called 'field coal' – which is actually dried cow pats. Once properly dry they burn really well, but you only find them like that in the summer and the sack was nearly empty.

I fed chips into the flames, then wiped my hands on my trousers before turning to prepare supper. Gwen sighed, pointedly, so I got up and went to the small stream to wash my hands.

When I came back there was another person by the fire. I wasn't concerned; he looked like an old

—

beggar, the kind that seem to wander purposelessly around the Old Kingdom, begging for food and shelter wherever they can. By all accounts they could sleep on a rope and dine off sunshine, and anyway, Gwen was on the other side of the fire, and I knew she had a dagger in her boot.

"Ho grandfather," I said cheerily, shaking the water off my fingers. "Are you joining us?"

"If you can spare an old man a piece of your fire," he replied. His accent said he was from Varese, in the far north of the Old Kingdom, and was crumbly and uncertain with age. There was a gravelly edge to it too, and I wondered if his time in service to the King had been in the coal mines of Lenmar. I smiled. Gwen's grandmother had been from Varese, brought to Darriel by her parents as a teenager, almost a century ago.

"We can always spare a side of the fire for an honest traveller grandfather," I said. "And a bite to eat?"

—

"Would be right welcome," he said, sitting on a convenient flat log with a tentative movement. "I've had naught but berries and fungus these last few days, and some bread would silence the growling." He touched his stomach through his sack-like clothing. The way it flattened showed me that he had other layers on beneath his shabby jacket. I was glad – I'm always happy to be generous when I can, but I didn't have any clothes to spare, at least not here.

I set the stew to bubbling in our little black iron pot, and the smell of venison and potatoes made my stomach grumble too. Gwen brought out a coarse loaf; it was a little dry, but perfect for soaking up the rich gravy.

"Where are you travelling?" The beggar asked this in an off-hand way, just opening the conversation.

"Back to Darriel," Gwen replied. "We've been at the market in Pallin."

"That's a long step in this poor weather," he

—

replied. He may have smiled but his mouth was lost in the grey thicket of his unkempt beard.

"It's a long step any time, but especially with these floods," Gwen replied. "Four days on the road each way, but our produce sells for ten times as much in Pallin as it does in the local villages."

"A wise journey then," he said, sipping from a clay beaker of small beer I'd given him. He sighed. "This is very fine," he said, raising the beaker slightly.

"Tobias is a fine brewer," replied Gwen.

"And Gwen is a fine distiller," I replied. "Strong drink may be a deceiver, but the nobles of Pallin like her brandy very much."

We all chuckled, which told me that even if the old man wasn't a local, he'd been around here for quite a while. There are no true nobles in Pallin, not for a century and more, and their role has been taken by the smug and overfed merchants who cluster around the

—

Administrator like flies around a dung heap. Their aspirations to nobility were a cause of derision and amusement far and wide.

"So now you have our names, grandfather," I said, stirring the pot with a long spoon, "do you have a name we might know?"

"I do," he said, "but it is worn a little thin with use, so I am usually known as Reisija."

So, he didn't want to give us his real name – Reisija just means 'traveller' in Varesan – but that was fine. My best beloved's name is actually Dodorian Bolwen Gwenifer Hara-An-Dol, so she goes by 'Gwen'.

The only time my full name ever got used was once by a Priest on my Naming Day, again when I married Gwen, and by my mother every time I did something wrong when I was a kid.

"And where do you journey grandfather?" I asked, setting the stew into bowls and handing them out.

—

Gwen gave the usual blessing of those who receive food without having to prepare it. The old man just smiled.

"I have a great journey Tobias, but I am in no hurry to make it. I have travelled a long time and to many places. But just now I am going to Torreon." I nodded. Torreon was a village another week the other side of Darriel.

"Then you could stay with us grandfather, and ride the cart as far as the farm. Maybe even rest in a house for a few days – this is poor weather for sleeping out and the floods have taken a lot of the ground."

"I would be grateful for that *Sur* Tobias," he said, giving me a title far more than I would ever be entitled to. "But I have a different path to take this day," he said, his voice sad. He reached into my cooking supplies and brought out the salt box, almost as if he'd known where it was in advance, and sprinkled a little on his food.

"To seem the farm again would be a wonderful

—

thing, but I...," he trailed off. "Not at this time," he said,
"but I thank you for your kind offer."

We ate in silence for a moment, and I wondered
what he had done that he couldn't come with us.
Gwen's uncle, who owns the farm, is as law abiding a
soul as you can name, and very protective of his family
and the people who work for him. But the old man had
to have done something very serious indeed before he
would call for a Summoner to be brought. Sometimes he
seemed more fervent than even us in his desire to
protect our daughter Polly and her baby brother Gils,
especially since Yonne, his twin, had died so young.

"As you wish," said Gwen. I could tell that she
was a curious as I was about it. The stew finished, she
offered the last of the apples to him and a bite of cheese,
which the old man took. When he didn't think we were
looking he stowed them in his small pack. In this
flooded landscape food would be even harder to find

—

than normal, and I decided to give him our last loaf and a bag of dried apricots when we parted.

We talked of the road and the farm, the small things of everyday life, as the warmth of the fire pushed some of the chill out of the air as sunset approached. The flames flickered and I glanced at the stack of logs, but they hadn't been there long enough to make them even slightly dry. Nevertheless, the old man lifted a log the size of my leg with negligent strength and laid it over the flames.

"We'll get some smoke from that grandfather," I said, but he smiled and shook his head.

"It's been waiting for you for too long to do that," he said absently. The fire rose with a bright crackling flame that lit the trees around us with a vivid flickering that unsettled the horses. The old man stood up and ran his hand along Bracken's neck to calm him. The horse snuffled his hand and whickered softly, relaxing under

—

his touch.

"There are more floods to come," he said. He looked at the darkening sky. "The spring rains will be reluctant to leave this year Tobias," he said, his voice absent and his eyes far away. "The grains for your brewing will be hard to find for a season or two. More expensive when you can, like all your food will be."

The last of the westering sun touched the surface of the flood waters, the ripples making shapes that hinted at something recognisable before dissolving into a shimmer like oil on milk.

Gwen stirred and smiled slightly. "Have you studied weather lore grandfather?"

He shrugged. "I have been out in the weather for long enough to know what it's thinking." He touched Fern, and both horses fell quiet, standing hip-shotten in the warmth of the fire. I lifted another log onto the flames, and this one did smoke. Reisija glanced at it, just

—

as the last of the billowing faded.

"Your children will be pleased to see you when you get home," he said. This gave me pause – we hadn't told him that we had any children, and while Gwen and I are both happy to wear the usual 'bride markers', she will not braid her Child Rings in her hair as is customary. She says the noise of the polished bone rings ticking together as she walks annoys her. "Have you thought what your lives would have been like if your children had…come out differently?"

"No," said Gwen firmly. "I have not thought about it and I have no intention of doing so. But I do have a question."

"Yes?" I said, but she wasn't looking at me. Reisija smiled in a benign, fairly unfocussed way, as if his mind was a long way off somewhere.

Gwen pointed to the shadowy figures who

—

seemed to be walking, dry shod, across the surface of the flood waters. "Who are they?"

"*Kirin*," said the old man, "but don't worry, they aren't here for you. In fact," he went on, "I don't think they can even see you."

I hoped he was right. The *Kirin* are like ghosts, but not of the dead. They are the spirits of a place, or a season or any definite, natural thing. The local Scholar told us that they are a personification, ones that arise when the thing that they personify is under threat, or in danger. I think that was what he said – it made sense when he explained it. But the key thing is that they are never harmful unless crossed, even though they are occasionally startling.

"Are they here for you?" Gwen asked. On our seeming island in the flood, and with the thick night closing around us we could not flee, nor even withdraw so they could pass unchallenged. One does not interfere

—

with the *Kirin* on pain of something really unpleasant happening. The Scholar wasn't very clear about the details of that bit.

"For me, no." He laughed, sounding younger than he had before. "Because of me, yes. The *Kirin* do not care for the intrusions of such as me."

Reisija was not just an old beggar on the road, that was obvious. There are less kindly spirits than the *Kirin* in the world, and I was wondering what we'd invited to share our hearth. Gwen carefully moved around so the fire was between her and the old man. I reached into the wagon and laid my hand on the long iron bar that we carry to help us lever things when the wagon gets stuck.

The old man smiled. "Fire and iron, is it?" His accent was much more local now, younger, and his beard was a little more than a tidied fuzz on his chin. "You will not need that. I am no threat." He threw out

—

the dregs of his small beer and tipped a tiny splash of water into the clay beaker and set it beside him.

The *Kirin* were almost through the trees now, moving as if the great old trunks didn't exist. In their world, they probably didn't.

"You want to know my name," he said, no longer the old man who'd shared our fire. He lifted one of his hands to the sky and seemed to gather a little of the rich dark blue of the night into his palm. "I will give you that, and gifts in thanks for your kindness to a stranger." He reached out his other hand, pushing it gently into the bright flames of the fire, then withdrawing a piece of it, just as the *Kirin* swept across us.

Gwen and I were chilled to the core, to the heart of our bones, and the fire burned blue as the spirits of our refuge passed through and around us, and then they were gone and the fire burned red and gold, and the warmth returned in a gentle rush.

—

The stranger was gone too, and on the flat log he had lately occupied were an apple, as fresh as the day it was picked; a lump of cheese, pleasingly not as fresh as the day it was made. The clay beaker, now cracked, revealed that the water was now a diamond the size of my two thumbs together. The fragment of sky had become a sapphire as big as a hen's egg; the fragment of the fire, now a ruby of such value alone that I wouldn't have to brew another keg of ale for twenty years. There was also a Child Ring, and I felt my heart lurch sideways in my chest.

The name on the ring was Borazon Drew Yonnel Hara-An-Dol – the name I'd last heard the Priest intoning on the day we buried our son Yonne.

—

Hidden

"I wonder what they're saying about us?" We'd
been lying in the dark for more than two days, listening
for the sounds of pursuit and not hearing anything. Not
yet, at least.

"Pennycate and Baker don't sound as good as
Bonnie and Clyde, but it would be..." I trailed off. No
reply. The figure, so still in the darkness, radiated
disapproval, so I fell silent again, and listened. Nothing.
Maybe something.

"Of course," I said, "if you hadn't done that we
wouldn't be stuck in this shit hole. So this is your fault."
I stretched. The wooden floorboards in the old house
were hurting my back, but the isolated building we'd
fled to had almost floor to ceiling windows, so we'd had
to stay down ever since we'd arrived. The house seemed

—

to have been empty for a long time, so the floor was gritty and dusty. I was also convinced that something had died in there. The smell was not very nice, but Pennycate hadn't mentioned it.

Mind you, he'd not said much since we'd slipped in through a door we'd found left open, probably by squatters or tramps or some other incarnation of the homeless. We'd hidden our stuff in the cupboard under the stairs and gone to ground in a rush, convinced that the police were on our tails. Not yet, but I expected that they would find us sooner or later. Or somebody would.

The distant street lights coloured the floor a sort of grubby orange, which just made the darker spaces darker, rather than illuminating anything very much.

There were rats, I was sure, but that wasn't a surprise in a big old house like this. Pennycate didn't seem to mind. I suspect he likes them, actually, because when I mentioned it all I could see in the fractional

—

illumination was the gleam of his teeth and the curve of his smile, turned down slightly at the corners.

This was all his fault. The robbery had been his idea. The shop we went for had been his choice too, and that had not been any better an idea than the rest of it. Established shops had good cameras and stuff, he'd said. Pop-ups don't, because they aren't in the building long enough to justify the expense.

And pop-ups are sometimes used by chancers trying to shift dodgy goods quietly, and they would be less keen on the police looking too closely at the origin of any stock that they'd had nicked. It had made sense when he said it.

I knew who he was, of course, even in the dark of the old pub where we'd met. It smelled of old cigarette smoke and nervous sweat, and the beer was bloody awful. I knew what Henry Pennycate was about, and what he wanted. We all did. He was an incomer to the

—

local crime scene, a jack-the-lad hoping to make a reputation, enough so that one that the big families would take him seriously. He wanted to be robbing bank vaults not corner shops, and he was happy to do whatever it took to achieve that. He didn't care whose territory he worked in, whose toes he stepped on, who he annoyed.

But the pop-up, selling warm electronics for the shady Christmas market, had looked so good, and if he'd stuck to the plan we would have got away, free and clear. But he didn't, and he didn't tell me what he was going to do either.

"Why did you do that?" I'd asked him that as we ran, but he hadn't answered. The sound of the shot was still making my ears ring, and we needed what breath we had for legging it.

"Why did you do that?" I asked him again, lying in the gritty darkness. His hands suggested he was

—

waving away the question. Whatever, he refused to answer. "They're going to be looking for both of us, you know that, don't you?"

I was sure he did, and I was equally sure he didn't care. Because he'd done what he'd actually gone there to do, which I promise you was not to rip off a load of dodgy iPads and not-very-smart phones. Sometimes I can be a bit slow, and I don't realise what's happening until a long time after the event.

"I don't really blame you," I said. "It was just an unfortunate that you had to do it just then." This was a big concession on my part, but it produced no reaction at all, which I found disappointing. "I mean, you know that doing that wasn't what I signed up for, not something I wanted to get involved in, but that didn't stop you, did it?" I looked over at him, a shape in the darkness. His eyes were a glimmer in the lamplight. I'd been so angry when I realised what he'd done. I'm

—

surprised he was looking a bit stunned.

There was definitely some noise outside now, hunting feet moving carefully toward the house. I didn't know if this was police or the family of the man he'd killed. I slid sideways toward him and his leg moved. The disturbance in the air raised the smell again, stale shit and something old, corrupted by time. A torch beam, splayed by a searcher stumbling in the gardens of the isolated house, tracked across the interior and on to the ceiling. The walls had faded and sagging wallpaper, touched with mildew and darkened by damp.

The light flickered through the doorway at the rear and a muttered exclamation from the back garden suggested that other searchers homing in on us had seen it too.

"What do you think Henry? Out the front to the police, to get banged up for murder, or out the back into the arms of the family of the man you shot? Not much

—

of a choice really."

On the whole, I was favouring the police, because the local crime family whose head he'd murdered we're going to be much harder to walk away from. "Come on then," I said, slapping his arm. "If we can set them to fighting each other then maybe we can slip away."

Henry didn't answer, even when the front door caved in and armed police officers surrounded us. I suppose if I wanted his help, I shouldn't have shot him when we first got into the house.

—

BUSTER

Buster had come down with a bad case of lumps several months before. The vet had done tests and declared that it was cancer. Buster would be fine for a while, but then it would get bad and it would be time for him to go. When we decided that it time had arrived we walked the three miles to the vet and I cried all the way home in the taxi.

Julie offered me beer, which I accepted, and a puppy, which I didn't. I'd never thought of myself as overly sentimental, but Buster was a one off – just like everybody else's one off. He could occasionally be devastatingly intelligent for such as otherwise stupid dog, and knew exactly emotional buttons to push to get what he wanted – food, a walk, that sort of thing. He used to try to sleep on me, but Buster was a Boxer, and

—

weighed nearly as much as a small pony, so out of fear

for my circulation and the structural integrity of my

skeleton I restricted him to resting his head on my lap.

Anyway, by the time I'd finally got all the hairs

off the sofa, Buster had been gone for about six weeks.

The vet had disposed of the remains and I had

consigned him to nirvana or wherever good dogs go.

The house was starting to look less comprehensively

rumpled than it had for some years, and I found I could

leave my shoes out without getting them eaten. Julie

made me tidy them away when she found that they were

all lying in the hall and the shoe cupboard now only

contained one army boot and a rather elderly tangerine.

I found out that Buster had come back late one

night. Like most couples, we had got used to each

other's little ways. Buster would bed down for the night

by first prowling around the house for ten minutes or so,

wuffing suspiciously at spiders. Friends sleeping on the

—

couch would be treated to the full 'Hound of the Baskervilles' routine until I told him to shut up.

Then he would climb onto the empty side of the bed and fall asleep with a huge sigh. The only time he didn't was when Julie was there. Even then he would try, earning the nickname 'Goosedog'. It's hard to get amorous when somebody in the bed bares his teeth and growls every time you move. OK, maybe not if you're married to a Klingon, but...

Anyway, it was Wednesday night and I'd just got back from the pub, soggy with designer water because I was driving. I'd locked the doors, turned off the TV, peed like that kid in Brussels and dropped into bed. Then I heard a single, familiar 'wuff'.

Now I'm not the superstitious type, so instead of fearfully diving under the covers, I muttered 'what the hell was that' and turned over. The sound wasn't repeated, so I fell asleep.

—

The next night it happened again, and this time Julie heard it. She said it must be the gas boiler coming on. I lay there in the dark, wondering if I should tell her that the house is all electric.

I think Buster must have got bored with waiting for me to get the idea, because at teatime the next day he just walked into the room. I'd just got in from work and in he came, as bold as brass, but more transparent.

What do you say? I mean, he never understood a bloody word I said when he was alive, so what chance was there now, what with him having the additional handicap of being dead? I just sat and looked at him. He sat and looked at me. Then he got bored, climbed on the couch and went to sleep. Well, at least his attention span hadn't changed.

So there I am, trying to eat my dinner and watch something suitably banal on the TV while the ghost of my dog snores on the couch next to me. I knew I wasn't

—

dreaming – tinned pasta never tastes that bad in dreams – but I didn't actually believe in ghosts. Not until then, anyway. I had to accept it, Buster had come back. I read once that ghosts come back for a reason; either unfinished business (there was that half a tin of dog food left when I took him to the vet…) or because of some trauma or loss (I doubt the squeaky rubber bone I found behind the bath was that important to him).

When I came in from work the next day he was still there. I put down some of the meat I was cooking, just like I used to. If a dog's face could ever say 'pillock' then his did. I briefly contemplated killing something so he could eat the ghost, but then realised I was being daft. Daft! I'm standing in the kitchen with my tie at half-mast trying to work out how to feed a dog that's been dead for six weeks. I decided not to tell anyone, as being sectioned is normally seen as a career limiting move.

Later that evening I touched him. I was getting

—

quite used to having him around – either an example of the adaptability of the human mind or I'd just given up worrying – and I found him occupying the whole of the couch. Without thinking I said 'budge up' and tried to shove him aside, just like I used to. This time my hand went through. That spooked me. I had to have a stiff drink to calm me down. Luckily I had one in my other hand at the time.

Buster just glared at me, like Churchill quelling a troublesome general, and went back to sleep. I spent the evening sitting on the uncomfortable chair because I couldn't think of a way to move him.

What do you do with a ghost? I suppose I could have had him exorcised, but then I thought of the local Catholic minister, who had a face like toothache and the forgiving nature of a barbarian horde. I couldn't see the whole bell, book and candle routine working on an animal whose total connection with the church was to

—

occasionally pee against the wall.

All the other faiths seemed equally improbable, unless you count animists. I dismissed the thought quite quickly – the idea of a stockbroker from Esher who thinks he's a leopard having a go at shifting Buster seemed ludicrous. Buster hates stockbrokers. So I decided I'd do it myself. I sat down on the floor and called his name.

"Buster," I said. He looked up. "I don't understand why or how you are here, but I'd like to. Can you give me some clues? Do I have to do something, or not do something?"

He looked at me. I have no idea if it made sense to him because it sounded like drivel to me. He got off the couch and wandered over to where I was sitting. He sat down and put his head on my knee – the 'I love you Daddy because you know how to use a tin opener' posture. I could just feel a faint pressure and the

—

suggestion of warmth. I tried to pat him but my hand went through, which was freaky, so I hovered it next to his slightly translucent skin and moved it gently when I could feel the warmth. When I did that he sighed and gave that shiver he used to when I stroked him. He walked onto the patio, and in the evening sunshine. I could see the petunias through him as he turned his face to the rays. For the first time I felt tears prick at my eyes.

"I missed you," I said. He huffed by way of acknowledgement or possibly as a warning to a fly that happened across his line of sight. At that moment Julie came into the room. I wasn't sure if she could see Buster or if he was just a private hallucination, but her cry of surprise answered the question for me.

"Isn't that Buster? I thought he was…"

"He is," I said, taking her hand, "but I don't think he's noticed." Buster looked around and, seeing Julie, ambled into the room with that gunfighter waddle that

—

only Boxer dogs and John Wayne can do without looking absurd. The wuffed at her and she laughed. I was concerned about the slightly hysterical edge – I'd heard it in myself too often lately.

"How do you take him for walks?" Her voice was shrill. "Doesn't the collar just drop through?" Buster looked affronted – nobody can let you know that you've hurt their feelings quite as well as a dog. Apart from cats, but that usually involves claws.

"Oh, I'm sorry," said Julie, and then looked startled. Mollified, Buster nuzzled her hand, and I could see the flash of comprehension on her face as she felt the fleeting warmth. She started to laugh quietly and sat on the couch. Buster lay down beside her and put his head on her lap.

"He's warm," she said. I smiled and gave her a small drink.

"You get used to it," I said.

—

That was five years ago and he's still with us. We've even moved house since then. I was afraid that he would be tied to the old house, but he sat in the back of the car like any normal dog. I think he can become less transparent when he tries because nobody said anything, or maybe it's just magic. Or it's just what ghosts do. I don't know. We've asked around and read countless books for clues, but nobody can understand it. I think he just didn't want to leave.

When Sophie was old enough to focus we found out that she could see him too. She always calls him 'thin dog' because she can't say 'transparent' yet. Apart from the fact he doesn't eat nor need walking he's pretty much like he used to be, although he seems to sleep more these days. I wonder if being dead is tiring?

—

Sometimes I can't find him at all, and then I'll see a dent in a cushion and know he's there, even though he's being very thin at that moment. He's still being a goosedog, although that didn't stop us producing Sophie. One day he'll just fade away for good I guess, and go to those happy hunting grounds – although in his case it will be the happy snoozing grounds, full of sofas and sunny patios and petunias to chew and people who open tins on request and love you just about as much as possible without getting bitten or arrested.

I'd tried to forget him but he came back, and even though Buster, my dear old goosedog, will finally fade soon, I don't think I'll ever forget him again.

—

The Sulking Goddess

The teacher pointed to the board and slumped
into the drab lecturing tone that he uses when the
subject doesn't interest him either.

"It is claimed, in legend at least, that at one time
there were four seasons, instead of the three that there
actually are." I'm glad that he said it was a legend,
because everyone in the class was chuckling. I joined in,
but only because they were. My mouth felt dry.

"The heart of the year, the summer, fades to
autumn by the will of Belenus, our benign god." We
remained silent, as the respect we'd had dinned into us
since birth gripped our tongues. The fact that Belenus
got rather stroppy if you didn't was also a factor. "Then
great Beira feels the waning of the year and winter
begins. This abides as the gods dictate until summer

—

comes, by the will of Áine. The legend says that there was a season between winter and summer, analogous to autumn. There are illustrations of the season in books of fables." The board flickered to ancient pages, scratchily reproduced on the screen. "But analysis has shown that these are simply unusual depictions of autumn."

This made me uncomfortable, because the pictures weren't right. Autumn is about to decline and decay, but these looked like the new growth. We usually see this in The Burgeoning, the first sudden burst of life at the start of summer. Before it vanished, I noted the citation and decided that I should look it up later.

The teacher then droned off to talk about the Equatorial Smoke Stream that wobbled its way around the globe creating all sorts of weird effects that none of the gods seemed to be neither interested in nor prepared to take responsibility for. The idea of a fourth season was the most interesting thing our meteorology professor had

—

said for weeks.

*

Godsholme, the unimaginatively named home of the gods, was a well-known place but not many people went there. It wasn't out of awe or reverence, but mostly because what the gods get up to day to day is rather dull and they're easily distracted. Someone once asked Belenus, who controls the sun, a complicated question about orbital velocities and the sun vanished for nearly ten minutes while he thought about it.

People claimed that the moon was involved in that as well, and it was partly Cerridew mucking about while Belenus' mind was doing something else. Actually being used for once, one observer suggested, which was possibly unkind and disrespectful, but also accurate. I certainly wouldn't put it past Cerridew to do something

—

like that – she's not the most… stable of people. But I needed to find the missing season, so I went to the House of Lugh, which guards the entrance to the home of the gods. It's not quite a bus ride, but it isn't all that far from anywhere.

The entrance looked like the front of an office block, including the obligatory bored uniformed security guard behind the inadequately polished and slightly scratched desk.

"Yes?" The man looked like he'd long ago gone beyond boredom into the realm of stultifying tedium known only to the judges of amateur talent shows and sober people listening to repetitive dance music.

"I'm doing some work for a college project…" I began. Getting to see the gods wasn't so hard, but you needed to have a proper reason to do so. Idle curiosity wasn't enough, and any attempt at falsehood could lead to a demonstration that spontaneous combustion isn't

—

always that spontaneous. Lugh guards his people well, if intermittently. The guards' despair seemed to deepen.

"I've been asked to investigate the seasons," I said, trying hard to sound young and curious and as harmless as possible.

"Áine, Beira or Belenus?" He waited, hands poised over a small keyboard embedded in the desk.

"Well, none of them," I said. I explained the four seasons legend that had interested me, and he sighed.

"You'll need the Archivist," he said, tapping the keys with the enthusiasm of someone writing his own death warrant. Even his uniform seemed dispirited, but the document that was sluggishly extruded from the printer gave me the authorisation I needed. I thanked him, which he didn't deign to acknowledge. He pointed behind me and I found that there was now a door in the previously blank wall. You can't get lost in Godsholme, I suspect because they don't want civilians finding out

—

what they get up to most of the time.

The door lead to a corridor, which lead to an office, which lead to a little grey man sitting behind a huge, empty, grey desk. He looked like he was made of dust and indecision, held together with pedantry.

"Seasons?" His voice was also grey, not much above a whisper but perfectly clear.

"Yes please."

"Which?"

"There's options?"

The pale eyes blinked with a lizard-like slowness. "There are many, young man. The gods lay their hands across many lands. So, which ones are you interested in? Leto, Veson and Zima? Nyár, Osz and Tél? Kesä, Syksy and Talvi?"

"Oh. Spring?" I asked, my voice carefully coloured by uncertainty.

"Spring," he said in a flat voice that seeped

—

disappointment. "Very well." He pointed to another newly appeared doorway. "The Lady will be able to help you, probably. Good luck."

This uncharacteristic comment bothered me all the way down the long, drab corridor. I passed several doors on the way; the sounds from them were very domestic, TV channels showing game shows and reality programmes that needed no IQ to follow. I had no idea where I was most of the time, because the corridors are featureless and opaque, and in Godsholme the laws of physics are treated more like suggestions.

The door I ended up in front of wouldn't have looked out of place in a block of flats in a small seaside town. It opened when I knocked, and I walked down a short corridor into the main room.

"Hello," said the lady who met me, "how can I help? College project is it?" She was wearing a black and white twinset from a discount chain store and a

—

really nice scarlet cardigan. The pearls you would have expected had been replaced with amber in small, irregular chunks. It looked unusual and very attractive.

"That's right," I said politely. "Ma'am," I added quickly, just to be on the safe side.

"So, what do you want to know?" She gestured me to sit, and I chose a chair fractionally less stricken with chintz than the others.

I explained about what had happened in my college class and my need to find out about the origin of the spring myth. I didn't actually use the word 'myth', because her face became so thunderous when we both detected it on the horizon of the sentence that I switched it to 'traditional story'.

The glower started as a line between her eyebrows that deepened and extended as I stumbled forwards, wishing I could stop my mouth digging before I was completely buried under the weight of her tight-

—

lipped disapproval.

"So I've just become a story, have I?"

Her question sounded like it should be rhetorical, but I nodded nonetheless. "That's what's being taught ma'am, but I couldn't accept it. All the study I've done suggests… shows… that spring was just as significant as all the other seasons. Probably more, because The Burgeoning forces plants to grow so fast that they lose their vigour and don't take up all the nutrients that they need to. This is odd, because all the records suggest that this wasn't always the case."

She didn't speak. "I read about some tests that showed that extending the conditions of The Burgeoning over several months produces far better growth and much larger yields."

"Tests," she snorted. "Tests." The idea seemed to alternately offend and amuse her. She twitched her cardigan back over her thin shoulders and glanced out

—

of the window. "What's your name young man?"

"They call me Fitz ma'am. I'm very sorry, rude of me, I forgot to ask...?"

"Ostara," she replied sharply. "That's what most of them called me." She fell silent, straightened an already straight cushion on the brown damask couch. A trio of ducks on the wall twitched when the lead mallard eased a stiffness from one wing, then settled back into a flying position with what sounded like a resigned sigh. Madam Ostara didn't notice.

"The Archivist sent me to see you ma'am. Because I asked about... the historicity of spring."

"Historicity, is it? Well, I'm sure I wouldn't know anything about that." She sniffed. "I know when I'm not wanted," she added, which seemed to be another non-sequitur but probably wasn't.

I looked around the spacious room. It seemed crowded with things of no particular consequence;

—

china figurines that seemed to be watching me, framed mottos that changed when you looked at them, snow globes with what looked like real snow in them, and half a hundred other pieces of frippery. They encrusted every horizontal surface like the barnacles that flourish whenever Mac Lir stops keeping his shorelines clean. This happens a lot – he may be the god of the seas but he's an inattentive housekeeper.

It was like I'd been transported to the parlour in my aunty Aoife's house. It may have been in my mind's nose, if you see what I mean, but I swear I could smell over-boiled cabbage and lumpy gravy burning on the stove. The only display that looked out of place was a cabinet full of eggs. This wasn't an oological collection – they were mostly plain chicken's eggs, painted or otherwise decorated. Madam Ostara watched as I examined the mass – the more I looked the more I could see; there must have been thousands, in a cabinet

—

apparently only big enough to hold a dozen or so.

I turned away into a disapproving silence thick enough to fold, finding Madam Ostara glaring at me. Gods can, of course, look like whatever they want, but I had the feeling this pinch-mouthed middle-aged woman with a cheap perm and no dress sense was pretty close to the original.

"I used to get lots of those," she sniffed, finally rising from the couch. She was surprisingly tall and quite muscular. "The rabbits were my Heralds, the eggs their sacrifices. I was… honoured." The last word was tight and bitter.

I had a sneaking feeling that the Archivist had been less than entirely honest with me. Madam Ostara didn't just know all about the myth of spring – she probably was Spring. Gulp.

"We all have our aspects you know, faces we show to the universe," she said. "Sometimes they get

—

appropriated, or stolen."

I was fascinated. Most of the time when the gods speak it's gnomic mumbling and things so ambiguous that priests spend umpteen hours on television arguing about what it meant. I never understood why they didn't just come here and ask. "Are you Spring, ma'am?"

"Well done. You're the first one for centuries to work it out," she replied, and a little of the careworn sagginess left her face. The air lost its faint taint of abused brassica and took on the freshness of the first day of The Burgeoning, sweet and chill and full of unlocked promise. "Do you all still celebrate the feast days?"

"We do ma'am."

"I had one, but the White God stole it and gave it to one of his whey-faced virgins. They used to make a bed for me on my festival, and set out meat and drink. Now only that fat old fraud Claus gets that. I used the energy to fuel the rising of the sap and the plants

—

pushing through the snow. He just eats it and gets fat. I don't know how his poor bloody reindeer manage."

I remained quite still because, I promise you, she wasn't talking to me. The room changed as she spoke, the walls fading away. The ducks flew away with a grateful quack.

"There were other names for me of course, always other names. Some people called me Gefn, which I really dislike because it makes me sound like a sneeze. Another lot thought I was a bear. Do I look like a bear?" She twirled on the spot, and the walls were almost gone and she was dressed in a floating gauzy robe that flared like an opening flower as she spun.

"No ma'am," I said with total honesty. She didn't, she looked young and tall and strong, and I was wondering if I could find my way to a door I recognised when the room faded away completely and we were in a woodland glade, just at the start of The Burgeoning.

—

"I had a son you know, but that bitch Arianhod said he couldn't marry a mortal woman, see." She suddenly sounded very Welsh. "No idea why. Jealous I suppose, but my brothers made Llew a wife of flowers for him. Oak, broom and meadowsweet she was, with a touch of owls when the mood was on her. They live in Cardiff now. Llew is a falconer. Blod is a guide at the castle." She fell silent.

"Will you come back ma'am?" I asked. In her power, Ostara – Eostra as she was sometimes called – was a thing of glory.

"To be ignored, to have the White God steal my worshippers again? I don't think so." Dark clouds were gathering on the horizon, but the fresh flowers still smelled wonderful.

"Please. The world fades for the want of the hope that you bring." I thought. "New life doesn't quicken in an instant. A sow takes a quarter year to make a piglet; a

—

woman three quarters of a year to make a child. But

plants go from seed to full grown in days, and it isn't

right." I stood as tall as I could. "Ma'am, the world has

waited for too long for your return. Without your gentle

hand new life burns too bright to burn as long as it

should. And the world is dying because of it."

"And will I be accepted?"

"Once we're all over the shock, yes. Mac Lir

makes storms because he resents us putting oil rigs in his

oceans. Nauda hates wind turbines, claims they steal the

breeze. The Dagda has a thing about mines. Ogma will

screw with computers whenever he can – I mean,

somebody has to be responsible for Windows 10. So

yes, Brigid will be accepted again. Welcomed even."

"And the Saint that stole my name?"

"She has to take care of an entire country,

blacksmiths, mariners, printing presses, bastard children

and people who look after chickens. I think she's got

—

enough to do."

Ostara looked at me, flowing robes of black and red below hair as white as snow never is. "Who are you? Really, I mean."

My shoulders hunched and smoothed as my wings grew and I took on my true form for the first time in centuries. "Fitheach, ma'am. I bring you greetings from The Dagda and an honourable request that you resume your rightful place at his side."

She laughed. "I shall, My Lord Raven. Now let us return the earth to how it should be."

—

Haunted Holidays

He waved to me as I came into his office,
shrugging apologetically and talking into the telephone
tucked under one ear at the same time.

"Visitors can wear white sheets on this sort of
visit of course, but it's becoming far less popular – apart
from anything else, getting the fit right is murder, if
you'll pardon the expression. Chain rattling and heavy
footsteps are available of course, but only as extras."
Pause. "Well, portraits with eyeholes to look through are
always possible, but they might not be fashionable. How
many people have portraits on their walls in the day and
age you are in?"

He put his hand over the mouthpiece, mimed
'sorry' and returned to the call.

"No, I'm afraid that a poster of semi-dressed

—

motion picture stars doesn't count. Yes, we do still provide the 'appearing in photographs when not in the scene' service, but it is far less effective than it was. Well, in the days of film cameras people would print every image but now, with digital pictures, they take hundreds of snaps and never look at them."

He nodded, as people do even though the person on the other end can't see them, and I noticed he was using a 1965 model 712 telephone, more usually called a Trimphone. With all the possible models available to him, I wondered why he'd chosen that one. "Yes. It's all in the brochure. I'll send you a copy as soon as possible. Thank you."

He put the phone down, smiled thanks to the pallid consumptive who had brought me here from the river. He gestured me to sit at the other side of the desk.

"Sorry about that," he said with a sincerely plastic smile. "It's so much easier with our regulars – they

—

always have a clear idea of what service they want. It's those that are travelling for the first time that need their hands held."

"So I understand," I said.

He smiled again, leaning back in his chair. "You want to do a feature on me, do you?"

I smiled. "Yes. The Editor is very interested in the services you provide."

"Good, good. I have to say," he went on, leaning forward, "we don't get many like you here these days."

"Journalists?"

"Vitals."

"Vitals?" I made a quick note of the word. "What are Vitals?"

He looked at me. "People who aren't dead. Yet." I paused. Ancient myth made it sound like this side of the rivers should have been fitted with a revolving door. Apparently not any more. "So, Mr...?"

—

"Regis, Stanley Regis. No point in offering to shake your hand, under the circumstances."

"Quite." His fingers remained laced across the brocade waistcoat that covered his ample stomach. He was clearly not the victim of starvation or a wasting sickness, but I knew it was not considered tactful to ask what had brought them to this side of the river.

"How long ago did you start this service?"

"Difficult to say, really. When are you from?"

"Early twenty first century. King William and Queen Katherine on the throne, the Princes and Princess Sophia still at school. Er… they're on the verge of outlawing petrol cars. Yet another coalition government is ineffectually cluttering up parliament. The Americans haven't quite managed to reverse all the damage that idiot Trump and his sycophants did."

He nodded. "Yes. He wasn't made very welcome

—

when he got here, I have to say. It was Her Majesty Queen Victoria and Prince Albert and, oh so many children, when I first came here. So, I think I have been doing it for perhaps a century and a half, as you would count it."

"So how did…" I picked up a brochure. It was printed on cheap shiny stock with lots of stars containing words like 'offer' and 'special deal' inside them. It looked like a desperate take-away menu, "'Haunting For You' begin?"

"Well," said Stanley, "haunting has been going on for ever, almost, but it wasn't properly organised. In some places, where the barrier between the worlds is a bit thinner than usual, Uncle Tom Cobley and all were getting through. It was usually ruined castles, draughty old houses, clapper bridges and the like, and most of the time there was nothing to see."

"Nobody to see them, don't you mean?"

—

"Oh no, most people don't travel back to frighten people," Stanley replied earnestly. That was the thing about Stanley, the earnestness, almost as if he were trying to make something fairly trivial into something really significant.

"So what then?"

"Sometimes it's to pass on a message, to look at what their descendants are doing, but most of the time it's because they're bored. It can be very dull here." He sighed. "They try to organise activities, but people aren't motivated. I mean, why would you be? You have everything you could ever want and there's no *need* to do anything."

I looked at the cheaply panelled room, the posters typical of an under-capitalised and imagination-deficient travel agency. It made me wonder about the man who had set it up, and, more importantly, why.

"But I'm not the type to sit still when I know

—

something needs doing, so I sort of got it organised, see." As he talked Stanley became more substantial and, for no reason I could identify, started to speak in a slight Welsh accent. "Started out just helping a few friends to go somewhere interesting, then someone suggested that I set up properly, make it more professional like."

I studied the brochure as he talked. The headings alone spoke volumes, ones that Stanley apparently couldn't read. 'The Fleeting Glimpse – an Introduction to Returning'; 'Homing In – tracing your descendants and disapproving of their lives'; 'Techno Travel – communication from beyond by text, e-mail and other social media'.

"What about clients who want screaming skulls and things like that? They seem to be quite popular, even in the glare of modern science."

He seemed uncomfortable. "Yes, that can be

—

done, but here at HfY we offer a more personal service. If you want auto-haunts, or things designed just to frighten Vitals, then we suggest people go to Bettiscombe Hauntings. They specialise in that sort of thing." His tone was disapproving, dismissive.

"I see. What other services...?" He just looked at me, politely blank. "I'm sure you have some odd requests from time to time..."

He laughed. "Well, we did have one client who wanted to have a snowman melt and his face appear as it did."

"That's inventive. Did it work?"

"After a fashion. We organised it but the melting – which of course we have no control over – happened during the night and nobody saw it."

"Oh dear."

"We also get requests for faces on toast or in buns or to shape fruit in a particular way. We will try, but

—

they're very rarely successful. We once caused a tomato to grow in the exact shape of a client's head, but the person who picked it hadn't known them and used it to make a sauce without ever noticing."

"Oh, that was unfortunate. Do you have any special requests that you do manage to achieve?"

"Many. For example, sometimes Returners only want to be seen by one particular person. We use a Coext for that, but we pride ourselves on only using the most up to date models." Stanley seemed to pride himself on quite a lot, and he made the term sound slightly salacious.

"Coext?"

"Oh, what might you call it...a 'perception filter'. It changes something in the visual cortex of a Vital, controlling what they can see."

"How does it work?"

He shrugged. "I honestly don't know. Technical

—

Services developed it for monitoring... things, I understand. They give us access to basic models, but that's all." He sighed, shifting uncomfortably in his seat. "We do the best with what we have, you know," he added, clearly irritated.

I let the silence lengthen and watched as Stanley regained his good humour. "Tell me, Mr Regis, what did you do before you... came here?"

"Well, I ran a shop, see." It seemed to occur to him that 'shop' was perhaps too small a word. "An emporium of domestic necessities you could say, in Nottingham. My family moved there in 1850, from Bala. Regis' Requisites I wanted to call it, but my Elsie thought that was too posh, that ordinary folk wouldn't come in, so we just called it Regis and Sons. If you go to the city I'm sure you'll find it's still going strong." There was a kind of desperate bravado in his tone.

"I'm sure," I replied, perhaps with an excess of

—

tact. I know Nottingham, but I wasn't going to tell
Stanley that Regis and Sons hadn't survived WWII. I
wondered why, with all his facilities for visiting the
'vital' side of the river, he hadn't just gone and looked
for himself. I supposed because he already knew that his
sons had not survived the Second World War.

As I recall it was closed in the late 1940's and the
block was now occupied by three different operations –
a chain betting shop, a chain coffee shop and a
ubiquitous but worthy charity shop. All that remains are
the faded remains of the name, painted on the wall
above the frontages. The pub opposite still honours him
though; although it's proper name is the Parasol and
Bucket, or something equally fatuous, all the regulars
call it 'Reggie's'.

I nodded. "So say one of your clients wants to
visit, oh let's say, London, what would you do? Just a
visit, not looking for anyone in particular, I mean."

—

"Well, I'd get my map of the soft places out and ask what they wanted to see. Some want to go back to old haunts, if you see what I mean; others who have never been there want to see the sights."

"Where did you get the map from?"

"I'm not at liberty to reveal that," he replied with all the practised pomposity of a small businessman. He leaned forward. "I have a friend in Technical Services," he whispered, tapping the side of his nose.

I nodded and touched my finger to my lips. "I understand. What use is a businessman if he doesn't have good connections." He nodded. "Do you ever go back yourself?"

He was silent for a very long moment. "No." He brightened, although I didn't buy it. "I'm too busy here. Always a new service to offer to clients."

"Yes, the Editor did mention that."

"He's a good friend, he always knows what I

—

need," said Regis, "especially as we're launching something new."

"And what is this new service – I think the readers will be very interested in this."

"I'm sure. We call it transcorporation. Bound to be really big, bound to be."

"How does it work?"

"Clients are put into the body of Vitals and live their lives for them, if you see what I mean."

"So what happens to the er…. original owners of the bodies?"

"They stay here."

"Stay?"

"Oh yes. We can't do the transfer on the other side, so we use people who come to visit us." The door behind me opened and I walked in. There wasn't any point in protesting as I realised I could see the desk faintly through my own hands.

—

"When?"

"When you crossed the river – the Boatman is rather more than just a psychopomp." He smiled, suddenly like a shark. "The Editor was the first person we got it to work on. But don't worry, there are lots of other journalists here to talk to."

I groaned. I really was in hell.

—

BOGGART'S HOLLOW

"So this house is haunted, is it?" Michael started the tiny recorder as the car wound through the thinning suburbs. His editor had described the claims for the house as a centre of supernatural activity as 'a pointless and ungainly resurgence of a discredited trope'. He held it toward Lucinda. She cleared her throat.

"Well, it certainly has a haunt."

"A what?" She smiled at his frown. "Wait 'til I've pulled over. I'll explain."

The heavy car crunched stones as it rolled up the unkempt 'in and out' drive and stopped by the ornate courtyard gate. She switched off the lights and engine in one movement and turned to her passenger.

"Haunt is the general term used for a spirit that has remained in this world rather than passing onward.

—

It's slightly less specific than 'ghost'. There's a haunt in this house, plus one or two other things."

"Right," he said in a carefully neutral voice. "Who is it? The haunt, I mean." Lucinda opened the door and shook her hair in the turbulent wind. The promontory jutted high above the sea, crashing invisibly below, and Michael felt an agoraphobic lurch. The large, curiously angular building loomed out of the dark sky and appeared to be bearing down on him. He was enough of a journalist to realise that it was his own apprehension that engendered the reaction, and he discounted it.

"Every journalist who comes here asks that," said Lucinda. "Truthfully, we're not sure." She lifted a large bag from the boot and shut it with a brisk slam. "It's male, in fairly modern clothing and has no injuries that we can see. Dating through clothes and manner of passing can make identification easier, but without them

—

it's much harder. We're working on it." The gate creaked and Michael wondered if it had been made to do that on purpose.

The Reed House Hotel was on a cliff top known, with spectacular illogic, as Boggart's Hollow. It was said to be the most consistent and dangerous haunted house in the country, and appeared to be doing it's conspicuous best to retain the reputation. The sky grumbled with distant thunder and the sea shuddered at the cliff right on cue. Michael sighed at the self-conscious melodrama.

"It has been suggested that it was the last journalist who came to the house without a member of the society to look after them," Lucinda added. "We can't disprove it," she finished, with a small air of relish. Michael shifted under his green waxed jacket, feeling a cold line being drawn down his back. He disliked the air of mystery that Lucinda was trying to create, making him

—

more determined to get to the bottom of the mystery and why everyone was being so coy about it. If he owned a provably haunted house it would be wall-to-wall with television cameras – for a fee, of course.

"So why are the members of the Thaumatological Society immune to the danger here?" The gate swung closed behind them, and Lucinda's reply was partially lost in the crepitation of footsteps on the gravel path.

"We aren't, but because we er...believe, we are less likely to make dangerous mistakes." Michael remained silent as they reached the front door and Lucinda held up her hand. "This is one of the most dangerous points. Think of yourself as a visitor that the residents don't want in their house but can't stop, however hard they try. Consider the amount of anger that can generate."

"Sounds like a visit from my bank manager." Lucinda smiled fleetingly and without amusement. "We

—

are the intruders here. It would be unwise to anger the occupants."

"What do you mean?"

"I mean, don't touch anything or move anything. Don't even think about taking anything away." Michael nodded and took a photograph of the front of the building. Lucinda flinched from the brightness of the flash in the thick rain-dashed darkness. "Don't do that inside unless I say it's all right to. At least one of the things in there hates really bright lights, and may well attack if you do that." Michael looked at her steadily for a few seconds and then nodded.

"Right," he said in the same neutral tone. Lucinda glanced at him sharply. "All right," he said, holding his hands up in surrender. "I promise." She put the key into the ornate lock and tried to turn it. No movement. She tried again. Still nothing. With a sigh, she let go. Michael raised a sceptical eyebrow.

—

"Will you stop that," she shouted, and Michael flinched, but she was still facing the door. Slowly, and without her touching it, the key turned and the door swung very slowly open. "Thank you."

'Nice effect...,' he thought. His imagination had provided the building with a long dark hallway, drooping dust-laden cobwebs and an atmosphere of brooding menace. Instead he found a fairly pleasant hotel lobby, decorated in the style of the 1990s, with a broad staircase at the back and several anonymous doorways leading off. He wasn't sure if was disappointed or not.

Lucinda's torch banished the shadows as they stepped inside. He noted that the temperature didn't drop as he had been told to expect, and muttered his doubts into the recorder. She led him on to the staircase, and stray drafts tugged at his thinning hair like sly fingers in the darkness. Floorboards under ageing carpet

—

creaked and sagged at strategic intervals, and he cursed the imagination that was putting worrying shapes into the shadows. He was annoyed to find that he was trembling slightly.

'*Exposé,*' he thought, '*this is an exposé, and you can't do that to something unless it's a fake.*' The thought did not seem to help him, although the trembling eased when he remembered that he didn't believe in ghosts. He started to look for the mechanisms of fakery.

Lucinda led him up the stairs, following the pool of torch light. At the top she snapped off the torch and Michael felt a swing of vertigo.

"What...?" He began, ashamed that his voice had risen half a pitch.

"Shhh. Look ahead." Michael peered forward, seeing nothing for a few seconds, then frowning as the faint glow from one of the rooms on the long corridor

—

brightened slightly.

"Night light?" He felt her glare.

"That's the haunt. The rest live at the back of the building." Michael swallowed, hoping for trickery.

"Can we look?" Lucinda didn't answer, but started to walk slowly forward. Michael felt a wave of cold and clutched at his camera with clammy hands. As he neared the dim light the darkness began to press in on him, and something inside started to tremble again.

The room was empty apart from a bed and a tiny table. Both were bare. Behind the bed a faint glow, somewhat in the shape of a man, stirred as if in pain. Michael looked hard, but couldn't see the source of the light. He lifted the camera, but Lucinda put out a hand.

"No. Leave him be. You'd not get anything much anyway." The glow moved slightly and then faded. Lucinda snapped the torch on, revealing an empty room.

"Convinced?" Michael took a deep breath and

—

followed the torch beam around the room.

"Can I see behind the bed?" Nothing. "An interesting effect, and persuasive, but not enough to convince me entirely. You said that there were things here other than the haunt?"

"Oh yes. What is sometimes called a 'varien'..." He started the recorder again.

"A what?"

"Varien. We prefer the term - so much less vulgar than 'bogie man'." She stamped her foot. A second later a hollow thud came from the floor below. Michael made a dismissive gesture. "There's the boggart..."

"As in 'hollow'?"

"Well, this place had to get its name from somewhere," she said brightly.

"Right," he smiled. The darkness was now just a lack of light, not a terror in its own right. The house was a con trick. Nobody could fear it. "Can I see it?"

—

"No. It would be er...very dangerous. They kill anyone who goes near them."

"Really? If that's the case, how did anyone survive to report that fact?" Lucinda looked uncomfortable and annoyed at his bantering tone. "Any more? No invisible ogres? No ghouls with really bad breath? No more mysterious lights for your friends to shine up through the floorboards?" Lucinda shook her head as Michael heard footsteps in the corridor. She didn't look around.

"One or two of the other members came along, just in case you needed more convincing."

"To provide the bumps and the lights you mean," said Michael scornfully. "I've seen enough. More than enough. I didn't fall for any of that stuff," he went on, forgetting the trembling in his heart just a few minutes before. "I shall enjoy exposing you as a bunch of frauds. I've seen more convincing apparitions on a fairground

—

ghost train. As for the other things..." he didn't bother to finish the sentence.

"You're almost right," said Lucinda in an odd tone, "but some others actually do live her, apart from the haunt." Michael looked up at the gathered faces. Long teeth, poised to bite, made him cry out in horror.

"Wha..."

"Vampires," said Lucinda as they closed in to feed. As usual, she had done her job of enticing their prey very efficiently. The haunt looked on sadly. At least he'd have somebody to talk to when it was over.

—

Flowers

When you are the police, searching for missing children comes in two parts – first you have to find the kid, and then you get your hands on the shit who took them. This sometimes happens at the same time. Why they did it often comes a distant 3rd.

Joseph Partridge, aged 13, had vanished from his home in the middle of the night in the first week in April. His father, Terry, said he'd thought it was an April Fool's thing, but the fact Joe vanished on the 4th suggested Terry was either vague about dates, or he didn't care. In the incident room this was the thing that was troubling us the most, because Operation Gloucester – the search for Joe Partridge – was going nowhere quickly.

DI Gilbert was unimpressed with Terry Partridge's

—

account of himself. He isn't local, and when he gets cross his accent gets so thick you could use it to prop open a door.

"I am not at all sure that Terry is being honest with us," he said, tapping the picture on the board. The incident room smelled off cheap coffee and nervous sweat. Nobody spoke, because they all agreed. "He claims not to have noticed Joe had gone because the lad gets himself up for school, unless he mother drags herself out of her pit soon enough."

Dysfunctional families are a mixed blessing in cases like this – they're less able to be clever about concealing things if they've done it themselves, but they tend to have a much less regular lifestyle, which makes assessing their actions less straightforward.

"Terry maintains he rarely sees the boy during the week – goes from work to the pub, then home after the boy is in bed. It's like he couldn't care less."

—

DC Simon Gates raised his hand. "It's er…

possible that Joe isn't actually Terry's child. Eggie isn't

very careful… and…"

"Eggie?" Gilbert asked. "Really?"

"Angela, Joe's mother, is known as Eggie. I don't

remember why."

"Right. What do we know about her?"

"Age 26, dependent on pharmaceuticals,

formerly an alcoholic, which is supposed to explain

Joe's unusual behaviour."

"Foetal alcohol syndrome?" DS Hatherley asked.

"Possibly. I know Eggie was drunk when Joe was

conceived and was probably throughout her

pregnancy." He sighed. "I've been involved with the

family for a while now, so…"

"How does it manifest itself?" Hatherley asked.

DS Hatherley is a dumpy woman of indeterminate

middle age who would probably look the same on the

—

day she started to draw her pension.

"Poor attention span," said Gates, a thin, nervous man in a cheap grey suit. "Reduced IQ, poor coordination, sees things, claims he can do stuff he can't. He's hard work sometimes. He's a disappointment to his father."

Hatherley nodded.

"So what happened then?"

"Joe just vanished. Only the clothes he stood up in, no money to speak of, even though he saved every single penny he got, and none of the odd little things that he valued."

"Could that help track him? Maybe he'll try to get them again."

"Doubt it," said Gates. "It was flowers. Joe and Eggie are almost obsessive gardeners – it was part of her alcohol rehab programme, and Joe had caught the bug from her. He would help in the garden because if he

—

didn't he'd be alone in the house, and he couldn't cope with that."

Gilbert sighed gustily. He was obviously uncomfortable with this case – his own kids were much the same age as Joe and although he saw them more often than Terry saw Joe, it still wasn't as often as he would have liked.

"Pam, I want you to take Simon and go and talk to Terry and er…Eggie…again. Separately." He indicated a posse of horribly ambitious DC's eagerly waiting at one side of the room. "Terry went out and back in that crappy old van of his several times over the weekend, so I want you lot to comb all the CCTV you can to see if you work out where he went." He sighed. "I just hope we can find Joe before anything terminal happens to him."

*

—

Terry shifted uncomfortably when Simon insisted they speak in private. "You 'spect me to say summat I don't want Eggie to 'ear?"

"No. We just want you to be able to," Simon replied softly. "Because sometimes people do stuff they don't necessarily want other people to know about; whatever it is, we need to hear about it so we can find the boy."

Terry nodded. He was a flabby man with more chins than he was born with and a complexion that suggested a fondness for fast food and cheap lager in inadvisable quantities.

"Well, I ain't done nuffin wot Eggie don't know about." He rubbed at a long scratch on the back of his hand. "It's all like I says – I get up, go to work, quick drink after work then 'ome."

"You meet someone at the Shovel?" Simon asked.

—

The Malt Shovel was a drinking barn that indiscriminately allowed hundreds of people to get pissed with minimal supervision from ten in the morning until midnight, seven days a week. The local police knew it far too well.

"Nah."

"You always in the Shovel?" Pam asked.

"Yeah, 'cos I can walk 'ome from there. I ain't gonna get done for drunk drivin'. Am I?"

"Very wise," murmured Simon, looking at Terry with a weary gaze. He'd been listening to his excuses for too long to believe him anymore.

*

Pam Hatherley watched Eggie with considerable sympathy. With an upbringing as shit as hers, alcohol had been an easy and obvious way out, but now the

—

consequences were becoming clear. It was easier to talk to her when she was distracted, so Pam had gone to Eggie's house.

Eggie's face was blotchy, and not just from crying, her hair lank and in need of a wash. She did not, however, smell of alcohol, and had probably been quite pretty, once.

"There ain't nothin'," said Eggie, her hands busy with the pots in the garden shed. The movements – emptying, cleaning, filling, levelling – where done with an impressive automatic skill. "There ain't nuffin I ain't told you. I just wants Joe back."

"OK. It's just that sometimes people remember stuff they'd forgotten before."

Eggie added some sort of hormone powder – at least according to the packet – to each pot with practised accuracy. "I do forget stuff, but it's like I told Simon," she said, then let her hands drop. "Joe weren't

—

'ome on Monday, but that weren't nuffin strange. Some days he went 'round to 'is mates 'ouse after school."

Eggie looked at Pam. "I ain't well, ya know. I just falls asleep sometimes. I can't 'elp meself. Joe's very good, looks after 'isself when I'm ill."

Poor blighter, thought Pam. "He likes flowers?"

"Yeah, loves 'em. Says 'e likes 'em 'cos they're friendly, 'cos they look after 'im. Don't know what's goin' on in 'is 'ead sometimes."

"Are these his?" Pam asked, pointing to some floppy orange blossoms that she couldn't identify.

"Nah. Joe's into roses. Dark ones, like black." She pointed past Pam the scrap of garden that they had torn out of the sterile wasteland at the back of the house. The back of the bed was full of roses, healthily budding dark reds and purples, the freshly turned soil dark and rich below the thorny stems. In front were more modest, lower growing plants like begonia and tulips.

—

"Them's mine," said Eggie. "Joe can't do soft stems – he's not so good with 'is 'ands, so they get broken. He's happier wiv woody stems, things its harder to break."

"It is very beautiful," said Pam sincerely. "What does Terry think of it?"

"He don't care. Says if we want to spend our time on this, he's goin' to the pub." She stabbed a dibber into a bag of compost. "Like 'e ever does anythin' else."

"Would he want to go to the pub if you didn't grow flowers?" Pam asked softly.

Eggie snorted. "If Terry's awake 'e wants to go to the pub. We can't 'ave booze in the 'ouse, 'cos I'm ill, ya know."

Pam nodded, watching Eggie with both sympathy and concern.

*

—

"Nothing on the 4th," said DC Bland, who had been wading through the CCTV with a grim determination, "but he doesn't conform to his habitual route on the 5th, whatever he may have said to you." Simon Gates, who had done the first interviews, had failed to mention this. DI Gilbert assumed that was because Terry had failed to mention it to him.

"How much time is unaccounted for?" DI Gilbert asked. He knew Bland had found something when the swearing had stopped.

"Well over an hour. Probably more than an hour and a half."

Gilbert nodded. "Right. Seize his van and turn it over to forensics." Bland nodded. "Why didn't Simon spot this? I bloody knew something odd was going on," said Gilbert. It was unlike Gates to be that careless.

—

Terry sat in the interview room looking sullen. He looked like he'd been in a fight; both his hands and one side of his face were covered in long scratches that beaded with blood every time he touched them.

"So Terry, you got something you want to tell us? Gilbert asked.

"No."

"You told us you followed the same routine every day, but we've got CCTV footage that shows that you didn't on the 5th. Care to explain why?"

"No."

Gilbert carefully didn't sigh. "Terry, all we're trying to do is find Joe. If you were doing something you don't want us to know about, don't worry. As long as we can place you somewhere, it doesn't matter what you were up to." Or it doesn't right now, he thought.

—

Terry shook his head and winced, glancing at the blood on his fingers and frowning. Gilbert gave him a tissue, which he dabbed at the scratches. He seemed puzzled. "I ain't done nuffin."

"So where did you go Terry?"

"Nowhere."

"Did you go somewhere with Joe?"

"No."

"Did you see Joe that day?"

"N... no." Terry stuttered slightly and pressed his hand to his arm. Blood welled up through his fingers. Gilbert couldn't see how the injury had happened; nobody was anywhere near Terry, had even reached toward him. The long scratch that drew itself up Terry's arm was deep and gaping and the blood was bright red. "What the fuck...?"

"We need a medic," said Gilbert to Gates, and the younger man sprinted from the room. The people

—

watching from the observation suite had made the call before he'd even got to his feet.

*

Pam had been thinking about Eggie's garden, and the colour of the soil in the rose bed, so she had spoken to Scene of Crime. They had gathered a small group of people who understood respect for plants, who had moved Joe's roses and dug through the loose soil very carefully. It hadn't taken them long to find the wrapping and the cold fingers that had grasped a handful of plastic and soil before they fell dead.

*

The paramedics arrived less than five minutes after they were called, and Gilbert watched in silence

—

as they tried to keep Terry alive. The cuts on his face and neck were growing longer and deeper, even as they tried to staunch them. Terry had writhed for a few minutes, but then slumped as the loss of blood made him waxen and immobile. Then he started to choke, pawing at his neck even as the doctor arrived. She was in the room only long enough to lay one hand on Terry's arm before his body stiffened, then slumped.

She reached into Terry's lifeless throat and pulled out the black rose that had cut off his windpipe. It was tinged with blood, and the smell was overwhelming in the hushed room.

DI Gilbert looked up from the Scene of Crime report on the recovery of Joe's body as Simon Gates stared in horror at the long scratch that drew itself down his arm.

—

Messages

Weird stuff doesn't care about what it gets in the way of. It was a Friday in early May, so the evenings were getting longer and lighter and a little warmer, so people aren't wearing as many clothes as they would be in January, or Iceland.

I'd been in our local pub, the Slug and Bucket, when I'd met this new girl. She'd just moved into the area, she said, and she seemed quite interested, and interesting. Before long we were getting on like a house on fire and we decided to go back to my place for 'coffee'. Her name was Leia and, yes, her brother was called Luke and, no, she still hasn't forgiven her parents. We walked slowly through the gathering dusk, enjoying the absence of the biting wind.

I'd tidied up the flat before I came out, because

—

you never know, right? I'd cleared the answerphone too, because I didn't want anyone to hear my mum nagging me about stuff, so when we got in and there was a light blinking I knew it was a new message. I was all for leaving it but Liea said she needed to use the loo so I pressed the play button while she was out of the room.

"Hey, it's Daniel. Long time, and all that. Give me a call man – got some catching up to do. *Ciao.*" According to Leia I was staring up the phone like it was a venomous snake when she came back into the room.

"What's up?" Her voice was slightly deep, with kind of smoky sexiness that made me sweat slightly.

I played the message again. "You aren't gonna call him right now, are you?" She turned the dimmer down a little and let the orange glow from the street lamp outside warm the room, which made her coffee-coloured skin glow.

"I can't," I said faintly. "I ain't got his number."

—

"You can get it from the phone," she said, frowning. She pressed buttons and it said a number. I didn't know you could do that.

"That's mum. She called yesterday."

"That's interesting," she replied. "Do any of your mates know it?"

"They can't." Every idea of getting... friendly had gone, and I was feeling cold and slightly shivery.

"Why not?"

"Daniel died two months ago." If I'd had the wit to think about it, I should have expected her to be suspicious, to think it was a joke or a wind up or something. But she didn't. I never spotted that bit of oddness in all the other weird shit that was going on. She didn't stay that night; I didn't either – mum was a bit surprised to find me asleep on her couch the next morning, but hey, that's what families are for, right?

—

I met Leia again the next day, in the pub at lunchtime, because she phoned me as soon I got back. I didn't remember giving her my number, but at least it showed she was interested in me, or that's what I thought anyway.

"So, anyone else trying to frighten you with silly jokes today?"

"How could it be a joke? He's dead; I went to the funeral." I took a shaky pull on my pint.

"You went to *a* funeral Spike. They told you it was Daniel's. You can't prove it."

That made me kind of angry. "Of course it was. His parents were there; they'd identified his body. They wouldn't..." I ran out of words.

"Okay, so he's dead. Fine. Which of your mates is best at imitating his voice? Has anyone got a recording

—

of him talking?" Her voice was calm.

"None of us are any good at it - his accent is more than a bit strange."

"Yeah, it sounded unusual on the phone message. Where was he from?"

"His parents are from Wales, but he was born in Ealing and grew up in Leeds."

Leia nodded. "Not surprising it's a bit confused then. Anyone got voice recordings they could use to fake it?"

"I don't bloody know. Nobody I know of. Maybe the police – he's been pulled a couple of times."

"Drunk and disorderly," said Leia. "I guess," she added hastily.

Before I could react to that, my phone began to sing – 'Private Number', which means one of a small group of friends is texting me. She nodded when I glanced at her, so I looked at the screen.

—

'You not talking to me, you grumpy git? Call me before I tell your mum what you and Keisha had just stopped doing when she came home early! D.' I nearly dropped my phone.

"Again?" Leia asked, lifting the phone out of my hand. She tapped out a short message and pressed send. The phone bleeped. *'Unable to send. Number not recognised'.* It's the kind of message they normally give when you put in the wrong number, but Liea had just pressed reply. She tapped another few things onto the phone before handing it back to me.

"Now that is proper weird." She stood up. "I'm just off to the loo. Do you want anything from the bar?"

"Another pint."

"Sure. You want lager, or something that doesn't taste like piss?" Which was a bit rich from somebody who was drinking fizzy water.

While she was gone I called Daniel's number. It

—

went straight to a message from the provider saying his phone was not switched on. I sat there, looking at my hands. I knew he couldn't answer. He was dead and his phone was smashed in his back pocket. He'd fallen a long way from that window, but he hadn't made a sound on the way down.

He'd fallen face upward, and I didn't know if he had been looking at the stars, praying or just staring at the person who pushed him when he hit the ground. Leia brought me another lager, which I drank hastily. Better that than thinking. "So what now?"

She shrugged. "It's your ghost Spike. You sort it." She pointed one finger at me – gold nail varnish, left over from last night's gold dress. "I promise you, I'm going nowhere near your flat until you've sorted this."

Today it was a bit cooler and threatened rain, so she was in jeans and boots and a baggy shirt, topped with a battered leather jacket with a small hole in one

—

arm. It concealed everything, unlike last night's dress which had clung like paint, but I thought she looked even hotter like that.

"Don't know how to sort it," I mumbled.

"The messages have got to be coming from somewhere Spike."

"I know that. I just don't know where.

"You tell me." She shrugged. "I've only just got here – you're the one who knew him."

My phone chimed as another text arrived, this time from someone who wasn't dead. *'Who's the bird?'*

I sent back just the letter L, which means 'later'. "Sorry. That's not Daniel."

"So he isn't haunting your phone then." She sipped her water, lifting her eyebrows.

The text music went off again, and I looked at it with a sinking heart. *'You'll have to talk to me in the end. Much to say. D.'*

—

I showed it to Leia. Still no sender number. Then my phone rang, but it went to voicemail before I had a chance to answer it, which shouldn't happen. We listen to it as it recorded. "Spike, you know who this is. You've got to do it man. You gotta say who did it. I can't rest until you do. And if I can't rest, I can't let you. Sorry mate, but that's how it is."

Leia reached over and held my hand. "Why don't you just tell me what happened. Maybe if I knew more I might be up to help."

"It was an accident, at a party." My God, it was hard to talk about this. "Just the usual crew – me and Reggie, Angie and Mo, Tim... Jojo and Jackie. Daniel, of course. Couple of others. The usual suspects, I suppose you'd say." I tried to grin but Leia wasn't having it.

"Daniel was by the window. I was getting a drink and I heard a shout and he was gone. Fell out of the window."

—

"Could he have fallen out because he was pissed? I mean, seriously. An accident?"

"No. The sill is too high. He must have jumped or be lifted." I'd been over this many times with the police.

"Pushed?"

"No. It was too high – were talking, like, bottom of the ribs on Daniel."

"Did you see what actually happened?"

"No." I realised I'd paused before answered, and Leia was looking at me, doing that one eyebrow raised thing. "Tim and Daniel had been getting into something over Angie – she's...she *was* Daniel's girlfriend, but Tim fancied her. Tim's a seriously big bloke."

"Bigger than Daniel?"

"Oh yeah. Daniel barely reached his shoulders."

"How did Angie feel about that?"

"Well, she's with Tim now, so..." I shrugged. My glass was empty, but I didn't get another. I suddenly felt

—

terribly sober, even though the rain streaking the window made me need a piss.

"Was Tim angry with Daniel?"

"No. Tim's a happy drunk, not an angry drunk. He sometimes makes people cross, but that's only when he tries to sing." That one did make her smile.

"Spike, seriously, what happened? You've got to get this sorted."

I stared at the beer-scarred table for a moment. "The only person close enough was Angie. They were talking – arguing – right by the window when I went to get a drink from the kitchen. When I came back he was falling. There was nobody else near. I need the loo," I said, but after I'd stepped away from the table I realised I'd left my phone behind, so I quietly walked back Leia was on her phone.

"Yes, this is DS Blake," she said, sounding brisk. "He confirms it was Angie Mackay. Yes. All prompts to

—

cease with immediate effect. Tell whoever was doing it well done, very effective. Sorry? What do you mean... never mind, we'll sort that out later." She looked up at me, showing no trace of chagrin or embarrassment at being caught out in such a massive lie. "Thanks Spike. That was exactly the confirmation that we needed."

"But..." All right, I should have guessed ages before, but it's a difficult thing to think about, your sister being a murderer. "The messages?"

"That was us. Nobody was telling us anything and we had to find a way to get through the silence. Sorry, but it had to be done. You won't get any more." She stood up. "If you've anything else you want to say, my name is Detective Sergeant Lisa Blake from the Manton Street station." She paused. "I wish I'd met you under different circumstances Spike," she added, which confused me. She then left.

I was still looking at my nearly empty glass when

—

my text music went off yet again. *'Thanks,'* it said. *'Now all you have to do is tell her that you helped.'*

"Stupid bitch," I said. Detective Sergeant Leia was messing about again. I looked around, but fortunately the pub was pretty much empty and nobody could hear me swearing.

'I'm not the police,' said the text. *'I've just been telling them what to say. Angie isn't strong enough to lift me that high. Nobody else was close, and I saw you watch me fall.'*

"I'm not playing this stupid game," I said under my breath, and made to rise, but then I felt the pressure of hands on my shoulders, even though there was nobody there.

"This is not a game," said a voice that was right next to my ear, a voice that could only be Daniel's. "This is revenge."

—

The Broken House

The man walked down the dark and unfamiliar
road, not quite sure how his feet had found their way
onto it. He was neither hot nor cold and the sky was the
colour of wet slate, without a suggestion of clouds or
sun to ameliorate it.

At the end of the broken road there was a broken
house, a single angular hardness in a soft landscape of
trees, their limbs as bare as barbed wire, and grey, sterile
soil. The broken road led to the house, and when he
looked around there was no road anymore. In fact, then
was nothing behind him. A grey nothing, shot through
with twisting shapes.

But now a light. The door to the house was open,
with a single figure silhouetted. The light was an
ordinary bulb, the kind that he'd had in the house he

—

nearly remembered living in.

"Welcome," said the person in the doorway he had no memory of walking towards. "You are welcome here. Come in."

"Thank you," he said. The lady who was speaking was young, with dark hair and flat dark eyes like unpolished pebbles. "Where am I?"

"Here," she replied, her voice like dry ice. "You've always been here, but you can't remember it. Too many distractions to be able to see clearly."

That seemed right, so he nodded and followed her into the building. The walls were finely grained, like the memory of wood. It was not a house, not a real house, one that you could live in. There were four doors and one staircase, rising into an impenetrable, repulsive gloom. Nothing moved, and the man waited. The woman waited, and a cold sliver of silence passed between them. When it was with the man again, he

—

spoke, his voice soft and troubled.

"What do I do now?"

"Open a door," she replied, her voice like angry icicles rattling precariously.

The first door was so much like the door to his home that expected to see familiar things beyond, but this was not his home. There was cold and ice and a bleak terror that made his soul shiver and his hands clench as the wind cut through to the heart of his bones. Such a grim place, white and featureless, with relentless snow that drove all thoughts from the mind except how to escape the numbing cold. He quickly shut the door.

The hallway wasn't warm, because it wasn't anything, but it wasn't freezing and he felt his hands uncurl. The woman looked at him, expecting him to move on to the next door. With a small splash as his feet touched the melting snow on the floor, he turned to it.

Beyond this door was nothing at all. A floor

—

perhaps, a surface that would take a step but beyond that nothing at all. Flat pale light, infinite distance without form or feature. It wasn't hot or cold or windy, it just was. He shut the door – it planted a worm of unshaped terror in his mind that the frozen landscape had not.

The third door opened slowly. Beyond was a desert, furnace hot and sandy, with scorpions scratching by in hurried angular rushes, and wasps the size of his hand approaching him as he stood in the entrance. A flicker of curiosity. He leant forward slightly and looked around. Despite standing in the doorway, he could see no doorway. He guessed that once he stepped through there would be no way back.

Again, the grey hallway, again the no temperature that was a relief from the sere heat. And the expectation of the final doorway, the only way the man could escape the broken house now.

—

This door opened onto a forest scene, and he felt his fear wane. He seemed to know this place slightly, to half recognise it. Through here perhaps he could find his way back to wherever he had come from. He couldn't quite bring it to mind. The smell of the place was like copper. It took him seconds to see the fresh blood and the arrow embedded in the back of the man who staggered pathetically into the clearing.

In the trees beyond him there was movement, something like voices. Another arrow flew out of the undergrowth, struck the man through the chest, through his heart without doubt. The running man fell, then rose again, face agonised as he pulled the shaft out, and then he ran on, ran with hopeless energy, and the hunters closed in. More arrows struck, but he still did not die. Sobbing in despair and agony, he rose to his feet and ran on again.

He closed the door with a desperate shove, then

—

looked around the twisted grey hallway, past the

repulsive stairs that were creeping ever closer, then back

toward the way he had come in. But that door was gone.

He turned to the grey woman.

"What do I do now?"

"Choose," she said.

—

Printed in Poland
by Amazon Fulfillment
Poland Sp. z o.o., Wrocław

54758317R00096